SOULKISS

SOULMATE SERIES

J THOMPSON

Faye.
love always win
Thompson xxx

Copyright © 2021 J Thompson All rights reserved. No part of this book may be used or reproduced in any manner whatsoever without written permission from the author except in the case of brief quotations embodied in articles and reviews.

This book is sold subject to the condition that it shall not, by way of trade or otherwise, be lent, resold, hired out or otherwise circulated without the prior consent of the publisher in any form of binding or cover other than that in which it is published and without a similar condition including this condition being imposed on the subsequent purchaser.

This is a work of fiction. Names, characters, places and incidents are the product of the author's imagination and are used fictitiously. Any resemblance to actual persons, living or dead, business establishments, events or locales is entirely coincidental.

❦ Created with Vellum

ABOUT THE BOOK

A quest to learn about the past is about to go wonderfully, terribly wrong...

Arianna came to Athens to study the ancient ruins. Daydreaming about her work isn't strange right? Even if the man who seduces her each night seems far more real than anything else in her dull, predictable life.

Arcaeus had done everything to prove his loyalty to his god. Until Apollo betrayed him. Now he's alone. broken and determined to find his lost love...even if his search will cross time itself.

PROLOGUE

The world of the gods, full of myths and legends. Some based on truth, some on lies, and some—well, some based on love. Based on it, surrounded by it, and dictated by it.
In this world, gods and mortals converge. Gods rule supreme, interfering in the daily lives of mortals. The gods love and hate just the same as mortals, and they, too, seek companionship and revenge.

Ancient Greece: not as beautiful and picturesque as the history books portray. For in this story, the gods demand sacrifices and obedience, and the mortals—well, they fight back. With a little help from Love herself.

This story is one of love and hate, with a touch of denial and revenge. It is proof that love conquers all, and that no barrier, be it time, distance or death, can keep true soul mates apart.

1

"Apollo, I bid you hear my prayers. Please answer this troubled mortal. I gift you with the finest wine, most perfect fruit, and the life in my blood."

Arcaeus grasped his large fighting dagger and sliced the lethal blade across his open palm. The long, shallow cut immediately bloomed with dark red liquid. Arcaeus clenched his fist and held it over the blessing bowl, watching as his life's blood dripped over the open, crackling flame. He closed his eyes and tilted his head towards the god's statue, and silently repeated his plea to Apollo.

Arcaeus had lost her. She had been sacrificed only two months earlier, and the grief... He hadn't been able to control it. He had thrown himself into the only other thing that seemed important in his life. He trained with a vehemence few others displayed.

His skill on the field of battle had become legendary, quickly earning him the honourable role of captain; a huge responsibility for one so young, but a task he revelled in. Still, at night, the loss of his soul mate weighed on his heart tenfold.

Arcaeus couldn't comprehend why his lady had been chosen. It had been a good many years since any of the gods, especially his own god, Apollo, had asked for a sacrifice, specifically a human one. Arcaeus had to be honest with himself; he had never trusted the god. It was a gut feeling that just wouldn't leave, one that told him the entire situation was more than just a sad coincidence.

No one had known about their love, as brief as it had been. They had made sure of that. Their meetings had always been secret, and they'd never been fully intimate with each other. Thalia had wanted to wait until they were finally married.

Arcaeus dug down deep to prevent the hurt that threatened to overwhelm him, but the memories they had shared, the time they spent together... His recollections of those moments were all he had left now.

Arcaeus hadn't attended the ceremony. Not by choice, but because he had been chained to the wall in his room by Cosmos, his second in command, who knew full well he would have fought Apollo himself to get to Thalia. Arcaeus knew she saw her sacrifice as a great honour and would have held her head high as she faced her death. His only hope was that it had been quick and painless, and that she had been granted entrance to the Fields of Elyssia.

Arcaeus kept his head bowed as he repeated the simple prayer. He was desperate. Life had become dull and mundane, and he needed to find the means to bring back Thalia.

He kept his true purpose a secret, as he could no longer trust anyone. His intense feelings of confusion as to why his Thalia had been handpicked out of all the priestesses at the temple was like a small, constant itch that just couldn't be scratched.

"Arcaeus, I hear you, mortal. You may rise." The god's

voice boomed like thunder through the temple, and the flames housed in the sconces rippled in response. The air itself was thick with power, to the point he could almost reach out and touch it.

Arcaeus stood, his head still bowed as he waited for the god to address him. To speak without permission was a great insult, one that never went without severe punishment.

"Arcaeus, you have summoned me. For what purpose do you command the presence of the Sun God?"

The god's voice was hard, with no sign of warmth or joviality; power laced every word.

"Forgive me, my lord. I call upon you as your humble servant. I seek your wisdom." Arcaeus let the words out in a rush. He knew only too well what the consequences of dealing with the gods were, especially with one such as Apollo, known for his vanity, cruelty, and ability to turn everything to his own gain.

"Speak of what you require, Arcaeus. I have much to do." Arcaeus, his head now raised, looked up at the god, whose aura was bright and powerful. Apollo didn't smile nor glare. He merely looked through Arcaeus, as if he saw straight into his soul, was tasting his deepest thoughts. Arcaeus was quick to reinforce his mental wards—a small gift he had inherited from his mother, herself a priestess of Apollo.

"My lord, I beseech you. I request a gift. The gift to find lost souls," he said, his voice strong and confident. Arcaeus was careful to keep his face blank as he fought to restrain the grief he held inside, and to hide that small spark of hope that bloomed within his chest as he voiced his request.

"Soul searching? Really, mortal, you surprise me. No one has requested that gift in a long time." The god sat upon his regal throne and looked amused by the request.

"My lord." Arcaeus kept his voice loud and steady. "My mother was the last to hold that gift. I wish to serve you in the same way she did." Arcaeus knew what the ultimate price could, and no doubt would, be, but the goal, in the end, was worth any cost incurred.

"Your mother?" Apollo tilted his head in thought. Recognition flashed through his godly eyes. "Ahh yes, I remember. Such a sweet thing she was, and oh so worthy of her gift." The god's eyes flashed again, this time with what could only be described as concealed anger. Its appearance was brief, a fleeting glimpse of emotion quickly hidden by a look of indifference.

Arcaeus nodded in response, his fists clenched hard at the familiar way Apollo spoke of his dear mother. His suspicions about him were no doubt correct, but it was not the time to dwell or worry about them.

"So, Arcaeus, you want this gift, this blessing. The price is high. Are you prepared to pay it?" Apollo's gaze bore through Arcaeus and caused the hairs on the back of his neck to rise in warning. A crackle of unreleased energy hummed through the air. Arcaeus raised his chin in a silent act of fortitude, his answer firm and resolved.

"Yes, my lord, I pay it willingly." Arcaeus calmed his breathing, his slow, controlled breaths bringing to him the smell of the incense he had lit earlier. The gentle aroma did little to soothe his nerves as he awaited the god's response.

"So be it," Apollo answered, loud and strong, his muscular arms raised. "I place the gift of soul searching upon your being. Do you, Arcaeus, son of Euadne, swear to serve The Temple of Apollo, and agree to the cost for this, so noble of gifts?"

Arcaeus needed no time to think. He bowed swiftly before the god, hope already starting to bloom within his heart and soul.

"I do, my lord. This I so swear on my life thread."

Arcaeus's strong-willed words made the god grin, his

smile no longer pleasant but predatory and calculating. The temple was filled with energy, and its power sent Arcaeus to his knees.

"Excellent, Arcaeus. I liked your oath. Fitting really, as that is the cost—when I have need of it. Your life thread now belongs to me." Apollo approached slowly, his immortal footsteps like thunder on the marble floor.

On his knees, his gaze on the floor, Arcaeus could feel the power of the god before him. A hand settled on his shoulder as the sweet aroma of ambrosia filled his senses, then the god's words whispered into his ear.

"I must warn you, Arcaeus. This may hurt—" He could sense the god smiling as he paused, "—a lot. But do try not to make too much noise."

With that, a fire unlike any he had ever known coursed through his body, and his back bowed under the strain. Arcaeus was thrown to the floor as pain radiated across his flesh, his mouth open in a silent scream. The only sound left to his ears was that of his god, Apollo; a happy chuckle of delight as he watched Arcaeus writhe upon the marble floor.

"Don't fight it, Arcaeus. It will only hurt more. I will leave you to enjoy your new…" he paused, his head tilting as if he were deep in thought, "blessing. Though I'm sure you will think of another word to describe the gift you begged me for." The god turned to leave, the delight in his voice adding to the pain and agony that flowed through Arcaeus's prone form.

"Thank you, *my* warrior." His laugh was the last thing that hit Arcaeus's ears before blessed darkness consumed him, sending him into sweet oblivion.

2

The moon, bright and clear, bathed the forest, lighting a path as Arianna meandered her way through monstrous trees of different varieties, all fighting for supremacy. She let her feet lead the way, her hands and fingers caressing the bark of every tree she passed. Soon, she found herself on the outskirts of a small clearing. White narcissus flowers were in full bloom, dotted here and there, and bordered an uneven trail that spanned the circumference of a simple marble fountain set in the centre. The musical lilt of the flowing water was the only sound that broke the silence.

She stood outside the clearing, hidden by an ageing oak, and let her gaze explore her surroundings, taking in every detail. Arianna felt the breeze and marvelled at the way it brushed against the small leaves of various colours, the season not yet set in stone.

Leaves the colour of gold swirled in the cool air and performed a silent dance with others of red and green. She wrapped her arms around her body and stared, mesmerized as they floated and flew across the clearing. The breeze picked up again, like a silent lover had caressed her skin, the temperature of its touch neither cold nor hot. Just perfect.

Her eyes focussed on the fountain in the centre as she stepped out from behind the huge oak tree, her body still hidden within its huge shadow, the shade comforting in its embrace. Again, her gaze swept over the clearing, and she admired the view in its simplicity. Her perusal was stopped by the impressive stature of a man.

Quiet in her approach, she let her feet again lead the way, surprised to find she didn't feel threatened by this stranger. The mysterious man had his back to her, his head turned away as if looking and waiting. Whether he was waiting for something or someone, she did not know, but for some unknown reason, his presence felt somehow familiar.

Strange, she thought, as she was sure she would remember this male. Arianna smiled to herself and took her time in looking her fill. To be truthful, she ogled. It would be a sin if she didn't.

He looked a hell of a lot taller than her own five-foot-six frame, and muscular, *very* muscular. She tilted her head and chewed on her lower lip, realising why he felt familiar to her. His build was all ancient warrior, like an extra from the film *300*.

She dragged her eyes away from the living sculpture that was his body and sneaked a peek at the rest of him. His hair was dark chocolate brown and looked silky and soft to the touch. It was an unusual length for a guy, but then again, who was she to judge. His skin, from what she could see, was tanned a fabulous, warm honey colour.

She stepped a little closer, her curiosity piqued. She was dying to see what his face looked like, more so what colour his eyes were. In her mind, she imagined them as dark, sultry orbs she could get lost in.

The closer she got, the more curious she became. Her

body moved of its own accord. She felt her heart as it thundered against her ribcage, its echo loud and clear as it hammered in her ears. She placed her hand over her chest, convinced its beat could be heard by the whole forest.

She frowned, her brain starting to question herself and her actions. She was swooning over a stranger; someone she didn't even know. All she seemed to be doing was gawping at his arse, and what an arse it was!

She sighed and threw her hand across her mouth, hoping he hadn't heard her. If her reaction to this guy's arse was this extreme, she dreaded to think what she would do when he—if he—turned around. No doubt she would make a fool of herself and pass out.

Either her sigh had been too loud, or she made a noise in her approach, because the stranger's shoulders stiffened. Almost as if time had stopped, he slowly turned to face her. Her breath caught in her throat as she looked at his face for the first time. Her initial assumption had been correct: his eyes were gorgeous. Deep, dark brown oceans that flowed with so many different emotions. She felt a little giddy as she forced her gaze away from his, afraid she really would get lost in their depths. After only a brief glimpse, she felt like those eyes were addictive. They had a pull she couldn't seem to deny. That feeling alone had warning bells ringing through her skull.

Her gaze now free from the hold this handsome stranger possessed, she took her time to indulge in the whole package that was this male. As she did so, her heart was quick to kick up a notch.

His back had been glorious, and his front was bloody magnificent. She could feel the blush creep up and over her cheeks as her gaze swept across his form.

His chin was strong and well defined, with cheekbones

that heightened his masculinity. And his lips... oh, his lips. She was riveted.

They were, in short, perfect. Perfect for kissing, with a full lower lip that just begged to be bitten. She felt herself lick her own lips, her mind quickly imagining what it would be like to taste his.

She could feel his gaze on her, and it burned her skin, making her feel itchy. She raised her eyes to meet his, finding his gaze holding a look of curiosity and determination, as well as familiarity. Frozen in place, she watched as he started to walk towards her. He closed the short distance with three long, confident strides, bringing with him his scent; a wild, musky aroma that just screamed male dominance.

With her hand still placed on her chest, her pulse accelerated into high gear, and her nerves made themselves known. No man in all her life had ever caused this reaction, and if she was brutally honest, it scared her stupid.

As he approached with a slow, confident gait, she took in his unusual attire, her mind quick to place the dress code. Her scholarly mind whirled in confusion. He was dressed in the traditional garments of what she could only imagine an Ancient Greek would wear. Most of his body was covered in a long red cloak, leaving only his leather sandals, as well as his greaves, visible. No helmet was present, a missing piece to what she pictured would be the full ensemble, but she would bet a month's pay that it was large and spectacular, with a full trim of horsehair. As he moved, she could see a glimpse of a simple chiton, but with a muscle cuirass over the top, leaving his bulging biceps free to move.

Continuing her perusal, her gaze became snagged on his hip. A large, lethal sword hung there, ready and waiting for its master's use. Confusion marked her brow as she dragged her gaze away, coming to rest at her feet. A myriad of feelings swept through her mind: confusion, attraction, as well as that annoying feeling of familiarity. Her eyes focused on her own feet, her toes nails plain in colour but encased in simple leather sandals. Tipping her foot from side to side, she admired the craftsmanship. Her fingers gripped the material of her skirt as she finally registered her own state of dress.

She gasped as she took in the beautiful, pale purple, silk-like material, which flowed down her body, its design traditional Grecian. She fingered the dress, lifting it up again to look at the sandals, full and laced up the calf. Wow, she was stunned. She felt beautiful.

She lifted her face to meet the intense, penetrating stare of the male facing her. Her eyes locked with his. He had stopped only about two feet away, but he looked on edge and eager to close the distance between them. His eyes flicked from his gentle perusal of her body, back up to her eyes. This time, Arianna was aware of the emotion held within their depths; a simple look of curiosity but intermixed with something else; warmth, maybe even tenderness.

Her own feelings, the main one being confusion, started to come to the surface, a small niggle at the back of her mind constantly making her think that she recognized this man. But just how she could have forgotten a man as hot, delicious, gorgeous and damn right lickable as this male was? She honestly had no idea. No woman, alive or dead, could forget his face or that body. Internally, she had already melted into a huge puddle of goo. But that feeling of déjà vu just would not go away, no matter how hard she tried. The breeze, as if called by an unknown source, chose that precise moment to pick up. Its caress swirled through and around them; it lifted her long, dark hair and whipped the tresses across her face. As if on cue, and in slow motion, he gently reached out to catch a wayward lock, and tucked it gently behind her ear. All the while, her eyes stayed locked onto his face. He was close enough that she could feel the heat radiating from his body, which, combined with his delicious scent, made her think of long dark nights, skin on skin, bodies entwined.

His deep, accented voice broke the silence.

"I've been waiting." His voice was rich, husky, and its timbre caused instant goosebumps to appear across her skin, followed by a deep shiver racing up her spine. She locked her knees, nervous and afraid that they would buckle. Gathering what wits she had left, she spoke, her voice slightly shaky as she answered, knowing she sounded stupid.

"You have? What have you been waiting for?" With a lock of her hair still trapped within his fingertips, he stepped closer, their bodies now almost touching.

"You, my love. I have been waiting for you."

Such simple words, but powerful enough to make a girl's heart stutter. Her chin lifted in an attempt to hide the underlying nerves and confusion that lingered.

"I don't even know you. How can you be waiting for me?" Her words rushed out, and the thought of stepping back crossed her mind, but she stood tall and fought down the urge.

His brows furrowed in confusion, and his eyes flickered back and forth between hers as if trying to read her. She looked away. She simply couldn't get her head around any of this. There were far too many conflicting emotions shooting through her skull. She couldn't make heads nor tails of it.

Her thoughts elsewhere, she missed his intent, until suddenly his lips were almost touching hers, his breath fresh as it whispered over her skin. And then he gently brushed his mouth across hers.

Her blood started to heat at his gentle touch. He pulled his head away, only a fraction, his gaze searching her face for any reaction to his touch. As if he sensed something in her body language, a tiny change that confirmed his attention was wanted, he bent his head and kissed her again. His tongue swept across her soft, pink lips as he begged for entry. Unable to fight the erotic pull of need, she opened immediately, giving him entry to the moist haven that was her mouth.

She felt like she had no control over her thoughts or actions as she stepped into his body, the heat and scent of this male engulfing her. She placed her small hands firmly upon his chest, the thin leather of his breastplate futile in its effort to hide the masculinity and strength held within. His heartbeat was equal to her own; proof that she was not the only one affected by the kiss.

And what a kiss it was. It was perfect, it was gentle, and yet, at the same time, she could feel his restrained passion waiting just beneath the surface, ready to be unleashed. Her earlier musings had been right: his lips were made for kissing. The intense pleasure of his simple kiss was almost too much. She could feel her knees weakening, so she pulled back slightly, her lips swollen, her eyes futile in their attempt to focus as she peered up at the warrior.

His hands rested on her waist as his eyes again searched her face. A small smile tugged at his lips. "Do you know who I am now?"

His quiet question was filled with concern. His hands tightened before he leaned in to touch her lips with his own again, a simple brush of flesh promising so much more. And she really wanted more. The thought shocked her. She didn't even know this man.

The suggestion that she would need another reminder was on the tip of her tongue when a loud, shrill noise vibrated through the forest. The silence broke, along with the erotic spell woven between them. She jumped out of his arms, her heartrate shooting up and out of her throat as she looked about for the source of the sound. The warrior, sword in hand, eased her behind him, his hand gentle on her arm, his stance ready to take on this unknown foe.

With her hands firmly placed on the warrior's back, she concentrated on the sound, before her fog-filled mind finally clicked and the identification of the sound became clear. She snorted loudly before starting to giggle. Unable to stop, she closed her eyes, resting her head against his strong back.

She couldn't stop giggling as she opened her eyes and turned her head. Eyeing the source of the noise, her hand reached out from the covers to switch off the alarm.

The best kiss of her life had been a dream.

Typical.

3

"Arianna, are you listening to me?"

Jumping a little, Arianna felt her face go beetroot red when she realized that, yet again, she had been caught daydreaming rather than listening.

But damn, the daydreams were good. Very good. The frequent fantasies she had been experiencing were always based around him, even though it had been three months since that very first encounter.

They always began with the same scene: she made her way through the forest towards the same marble fountain, and she glimpsed him through the trees. But that's about as far as it got. To be honest, Arianna had spent many a night and day telling herself he wasn't real. He was just a fantasy. But how in God's name can a fantasy man make a woman ache just from a dream kiss? She found that the most confusing thing of all. But then, if she was truthful, she wanted round two of that kiss. She wanted to see if it was as heated and fabulous as the first time. She wanted—no, desperately needed—to experience that feeling again. With her chin rested in her hands, Arianna looked at her best friend before she reverted to her inner thoughts. She wasn't surprised about her reaction to the dream man. It had been forever since she'd been on a date, and a lifetime since she'd been swept off her feet. Okay, scrap that, make it never. She found she just couldn't trust men. All they ever seemed to do was make women feel bad about themselves, try to change them, and then dump them because they aren't good enough.

Arianna's last 'relationship' hadn't lasted longer than a month. She could remember his excuse clearly: it wasn't her; it was him, and she deserved better. Arianna hadn't doubted that fact for a second.

It had been funny really. Arianna had found out that he was sleeping with another girl whilst he was still dating her... Bastard!

Though if she was honest with herself, she had never classed herself as man-catching material, not even eye-catching material. She had given up trying to impress the male sex years ago. She just couldn't be bothered with the hassle. Arianna kept her rib-length, chestnut hair tied back and out of her face, and she avoided wearing makeup as she felt it made her green eyes stand out too much, which, in turn, made her look just a little bit freaky. At five feet six, Arianna was dwarfed by most people, and she classed her figure as curvaceous, which also seemed to put men off, especially if there were stick insects in the same vicinity. Finally, another reason the opposite sex never headed in her direction, and why she had never ever classed herself as a 'girly girl', was Arianna was just more comfortable in jeans and a hoodie.

Arianna jumped back and nearly toppled from her chair as a hand swatted across the top of her head.

"What?"

She looked directly into her best friend's face.

"I said, are you listening to me, Anya?"

Arianna sighed quietly and sat up, attempting to concentrate. "Dammit, I'm sorry, Sonia. I was miles away." *With that hunk.* "Tell me again."

Sonia was Arianna's best friend, and her partner in crime when it came to their dream jobs in archaeology. With the typical body that most blokes would drool over, she was slender yet still full of curves, with dark red hair and perfect blue eyes. Most girls would be jealous, but when you had been friends for well over ten years, you tended to forget the envy—well, nearly. They had studied together at Manchester Metropolitan University, and luckily, both of them had bagged fabulous jobs at the Manchester Museum in the Ancient Cultures department.

"As I was saying, before you so rudely drifted off to another planet—again. Are you all ready and packed for our trip to Greece?"

"Greece? Oh yeah, of course I'm ready." *Not!* "I haven't finished packing though, but it shouldn't take me long." Arianna started to fidget with her hands, flicking her nails and pulling at invisible threads on the sleeve of her jumper. She just wanted to avoid eye contact.

"Good, because we are going to have a fabulous time, and you are so having a makeover."

"What?" Panic started to set in as Arianna watched the look of excitement flash across Sonia's face. She clenched her hands together under the desk.

"What?" she repeated. "Me?" She shook her head in denial, slid her chair back and stood up. "There is no way in hell you are getting your grubby hands on me *again*, Sonia." Her voice a squeak, she backed up towards the bookcase behind them, her hands placed in front of her in a silent gesture to ward off her best friend. She started to stammer, "The last time you made me over I ended up looking like a cross between Beetlejuice and the Mad Hatter, so no bloody way."

Sonia stood with her hands on her hips, red hair tossed back over her shoulder, and gave Arianna the 'look'. Now this look was famous in the museum, for it had been used for years to control wayward students, deal with arrogant professors, and con best friends into doing anything.

"Arianna Jane! I am your best friend and I have BFF rights, and you know it."

It took an awful lot of effort to stifle her laugh, but the woman made Arianna giggle when she had those tantrums. Arianna took a deep breath before she plastered a fake smile on her face. She knew it was easier to give up sooner rather than deal with a full-on Sonia tantrum.

"Fine, but only a little. Or else." Arianna left the threat empty. Her hope was that Sonia would regret any possible comeback and not realise that her mind had gone blank and she just couldn't think of an appropriate threat.

A bright smile slowly spread across Sonia's face as she rubbed her hands together. "Oh, Anya, we are going to have so much fun."

Arianna rolled her eyes and smiled. She didn't think Sonia knew entirely what this trip entailed, nor that they would be working—hard. The trip had been organized by the museum as a sort of exchange system; two archaeologists from the UK got to go to Greece and vice versa. All this was to build relations between the countries with regards to making the loaning of artefacts a lot easier. They had also made an agreement to let the museum loan some of the more special pieces in exchange for extra help on the dig.

Arianna was really looking forward to the whole trip. Three months of excavation in Greece. It would be heaven, for not only an archaeologist, but for a girl who had loved the Greek myths and legends for as long as she could remember.

Sonia wasn't keen on the whole digging aspect of the job. She was more of a once-the-stuff-is-clean-I-will-put-it-back-together kind of girl. Her job was to carefully piece the items back together; a time-consuming job she revelled in.

Arianna was convinced she was hoping, and no doubt wishing, to be sat on a beach for the most part. She couldn't wait to see Sonia's face when they got there and she found out how much of the trip would be work. She chuckled under her breath and eyed her best friend. Evil as it sounded, it was Arianna's little way of getting payback for the dreaded makeover that was to come.

Arianna stood up and grabbed her purse, perched on the end of her desk, and watched Sonia write her emails. Her brightly painted nails tapped loudly against the keys.

"Sonia, I'm going to head home now and get finished with my packing. Meet you at the airport tomorrow morning? Remember, don't be late. The flight leaves at 9am." Arianna massaged her temples slowly. A headache had already settled in as she waited for Sonia to reply.

Sonia looked up and grinned. "Okay, honey, see you tomorrow, and don't forget to pack all your sexy clothes for our adventures. I'm so excited! Sun, sea and sand... If I'm lucky, I may get a little of the other 'S'."

Arianna watched as Sonia waggled her eyebrows suggestively. Unable to stop herself, she laughed. Her best friend was always the one to lower the tone and keep her giggling.

Arianna, on her way out of the door to their joint office, shouted, "Bye, sweetie." She left quickly, eager to be home as soon as possible. Her love for her best friend was endless, but now and again she tended to drive her up the wall and around the bend.

She took a deep breath of the cool, crisp air the minute

she stepped through the main doors of the museum, the ache in her skull eased only a little as she slowly made her way home. Luckily, she didn't live far. Her home was a small, simple flat, located only about twenty minutes' walk from the museum. She switched on her iPod, slipped in her headphones, and flicked to one of her favourite groups. Turning up the volume, she hit play on *All your life* by The Band Perry, and made her way down the road.

Arianna loved her flat. It was her own little piece of heaven, set out just the way she liked it. Comfortable, bright and airy, complete with the personal tweaks here and there that were Arianna to the core.

As a child, she had fallen in love with mythology. Her childhood dreams were filled with images of warriors battling to save a distraught maiden, defying the gods themselves for her love. Real life, as usual, stepped in and taught her, as an adult, that those fantasies couldn't and wouldn't come true. So the daydreaming stopped and was replaced by the overwhelming need to gain knowledge about the cultures, and that had become her new love and career.

Mythological beasts, heroes and Greek inspired artwork decorated the walls, whilst a large bookcase filled to the brim with novels and research books dominated one side of the living room, the collection finished off by the hundreds of DVDs at the base.

Arianna dumped her purse and keys onto the coffee table, kicked off her shoes and wriggled her toes—plainly painted in a light lilac—into the carpet. Her aching, sore body finally started to relax after her long day.

"Right, Anya, no time for relaxing yet. Jobs to do first," Arianna grumbled to herself as she moved to the bedroom and grabbed the suitcase that had been thrown by the wardrobe in expectation. She quickly threw the clothes needed into the case: jeans, shorts, simple t-shirts in a multitude of colours and sets of simple, non-fancy underwear. Arianna picked up her favourite large shirt from her bed and ran a hand across the cheesy logo on the front. Comfort, that's what this shirt meant to her. The large logo was of a faded Flash Gordon dominating the material. She grinned and placed it into the case. She was about to close the lid when she remembered she needed a dress, especially if she was going to be subjected to a makeover. Arianna winced. The habits of her best friend were predictable, and there would no doubt be a date involved.

Finally, once she'd sifted through the rail about five times, Arianna decided on a long, light sea blue V-necked dress, with a high waistband. Arianna folded it into the case, zipped it up and placed it by the front door, all ready for the early start in the morning.

Changed at last into a comfortable pair of jogging pants and a loose t-shirt, Arianna grabbed a bottle of her berry cider from the fridge, curled up on the sofa and switched on her laptop. Finally settled and a little more relaxed, she started her list of jobs that needed doing before departure the next day. She had bills to be paid and post to be redirected, and it all had to be done tonight.

After she had stared at the screen for what felt like hours but was in fact only thirty minutes, Arianna felt her eyes start to droop. Her day had been long, what with briefing the other staff members on what would be required whilst she was away, as well as dealing with the usual number of students. She wasn't at all surprised she felt exhausted. Shutting the laptop, she placed it onto the coffee table and picked up the remote. The television flicked on, bathing the room in white light, the screen showing only static.

Settled back into the pillows, Arianna switched the DVD player on, not sure which film she had left in the player last and frankly not caring. As the film began, she smiled. Perfect!

Just what she needed to relax her mind as well as her body: a good healthy dose of cheese. Her mind sucked her into the film, one of her all-time favourites. Nothing could beat the original version of *Clash of the Titans*.

Perfect, Arianna thought. *Just perfect.*

4

Arianna had returned to the forest. She rested her head back against the trunk of an overly large Copper Beech tree and closed her eyes as she took in a few deep breaths. The scents were pleasant to her senses, the cool moist air filling her lungs. For some reason, this place brought a sense of contentment to Arianna that she hadn't realised was missing from her life.

Arianna never doubted for a second the motive of her feet; she let them lead the way, but deep down she hoped they would take her to him. Always in her mind, he was a shadow that lingered constantly, an itch that would never go away. Add to that the fact that in the three months she had been having this dream, she had only seen him fully that first time, which alone had started to get on her nerves.

Arianna's feet crunched on fallen leaves, and her mind spun back to their first meeting and how it had almost automatically become a permanent fixture in her life. A little alarming, considering he only existed in her dreams and subconscious. In reality, she craved the type of passion she glimpsed just beneath the surface. The restrained kiss they shared had ignited something buried deep down inside of her, and it was now simply too strong to be locked away again.

The breeze caressed Arianna's skin, and the gauzy material of her dress wrapped itself around her body as she stepped towards the line of trees that signalled her approach to the clearing. She placed her hand on the bark of an old giant oak. The rough texture dug into her palm as she leaned in close to peer around the large trunk.

Arianna already expected to see her warrior waiting. It was as if this time she knew the dream would be different. What she didn't expect was to see him facing her, a smile spread wide across his lips as soon as he saw her. Ever since the last time they had met, she couldn't get over how handsome he was, but now… it was simply amazing how much a smile could change someone's features.

Dear God above. Arianna felt her heart start to race. That smile… it was simply breath-taking. It radiated love and warmth. Arianna's step faltered slightly. Never before had a man directed that kind of emotion her way. For the first time in her life, she felt wanted.

Arianna paused. Her fingers clutched at her dress as she watched the warrior approach, a look of determination on his face as his long strides easily ate up the distance between them. Arianna shored her resolve and took slow, deep breaths. She would be in control of this dream. It was her dream after all, and she would not act silly, like she wanted to, like she was dying to. She would endeavour not to fall into this male's arms and beg for him to kiss her like last time.

He stepped closer, his body only a foot away from her own. The wind wrapped her dress around her legs as well as her own. His build was so tall she had to tip her chin back to look up at him. She would rather strain her neck than step back and show him, with action, just how much his presence put her on edge. Not from fear but from need. A need she just didn't want to admit to.

Their eyes locked. His deep chocolate brown orbs captured and trapped Arianna within their depths. The surrounding sounds disappeared, leaving only the loud thud of her own heart. Moments passed before the spell was broken by his voice, the deep, husky sound vibrating throughout her whole body.

"Finally, you have come." He let out a loud sigh. "I don't like waiting. What took you so long?"

He radiated power and heat. It seeped from his body like a cloud, swirling around her, bathing her body in warmth and his male scent.

"Come, kiss me." His voice flowed, just like his heat, over and around her body. Her heartrate, already at a gallop, skipped a beat at his question. "I'm eager to remember your taste, and the feel of you in my arms."

Oh my! Arianna couldn't think. How did he do this? How did this man know exactly what would make Arianna melt inside? No man had ever said anything like that to her. No man had ever made it known that they wanted her.

She took hold of what little resolve she had left before it slipped away and moved a small step back, creating some much-needed space; space so she could think a little more clearly. Arianna kept her hand palm up and outstretched, preventing him from taking her in his arms. His body language already showed his intentions, and as much as her insides told her to go with it, her brain was saying otherwise.

Arianna took a few more deep breaths, her eyes focused on his chest, on his leather covered, broad, muscular chest, and she shook her head, all the while berating herself in a small whisper.

"Dammit, Arianna, focus and get a hold of yourself." She needed answers, and she would get them. There was no way she was going to let Mr Studly and Handsome get in her way and distract her, but then again, he was so damn drool worthy. Everything that made her female jumped up and waved their hands, begging for attention as soon as she looked at him.

She took what had to have been the fifth or sixth deep breath and looked up, and again encountered his eyes. She was aware of his presence and strength, but his eyes showed his soul.

Her breath more like a squeak, she asked quietly, "What's your name?" Arianna kept her eyes locked onto his face. Only the slight tick of his jaw showed he wasn't happy with the question. "I need to know your name. How you are doing this to me?"

"I have no idea what you are talking about." His voice was so masculine, commanding and sexy. He made it continuously hard for Arianna to concentrate. The deep timbre alone made her skin break out in goose-bumps.

Arianna stepped further away from this male, and the distance brought with it an unknown sense of loss. She pushed her long hair from her eyes and started to pace. One of her hands tugged at a lock of her hair, the other gestured to the scene around her.

"Invading my dreams like this, making me... Oh, I don't know!" She stopped and faced him again. "Just tell me," Arianna pleaded quietly.

Arianna had no intention of revealing just how much this male was affecting her. His presence was like a tornado; it swept away her common sense and reasoning. She was definitely not going to tell him that these dreams had affected her real life too, and God forbid he should find out that since that first dream, all she had been able to think about was him. She had never been popular with the guys, but it was like he had ruined her. All men in her life now just didn't seem to live up to the image that was this male.

Arianna watched as he nodded, a small gesture of introduction, his own chocolate browns orbs never leaving her own. A small smirk tugged at his lips. "You called me. I merely answered."

Arianna frowned at his answer. Both of her hands now tugged at a single lock of hair, and her nerves started to make themselves known. She physically shook herself and placed her hands onto her hips, not breaking eye contact she rushed out her words, her pitch heightened with every syllable. "But I haven't called you. You're not even real. You don't even exist!"

Arianna started to pace two steps to her left, then back to her right, every movement tracked by the warrior. His silence bothered her more than she liked.

"You are simply a figment of my already overactive imagination." Arianna stopped pacing. Her steps unwillingly took her right in front of the warrior. "That and the fact I have a non-existent love life, to the point I am dreaming about men who can kiss my socks off."

This was getting to be too much, and her brain, already frazzled, had started to overthink things that didn't bode well. All that coupled with the fact that Mr Tall, Dark and Sexy hadn't taken his eyes off her since she had started to ramble and was now looking at her like she was lunch. Not that she minded, but she was not that kind of girl, no matter how hot, hunky, and lickable he was. Oh, and not forgetting how biteable he looked, smelled and no doubt tasted.

Arianna shook her head a little in the hopes it would help

clear her mind. A sharp jolt of the grey matter in her head might just remove the kinky thoughts floating through the interior of her skull and get her back on track.

She made the final few steps, and as she closed the distance, she mentally grabbed her big girl panties and hoisted them up. Her hand raised, she poked the warrior in the chest with her finger, each syllable she spoke emphasized with a jab, "You didn't answer my first question. Who are you? What's your name?"

The warrior, his eyes never leaving her own, moved slightly. His large, calloused hand engulfed her own as he raised it to his lips. Her knuckles the only contact with the warmth of the warrior's mouth, Arianna felt like an eternity passed before his gaze and mouth released her from his spell. Her eyes locked onto his chest. She could feel his gaze searching her face as he rubbed his thumb across her knuckles and over the area he had kissed.

Arianna took another breath before she let her eyes move back to the warrior's face. The look he gave Arianna was one of pure sin as he held her gaze with his own. His hand had a solid hold of Arianna's, and she seriously needed to get a grip and fast. The warrior smiled a little as he slowly released his grip. He lowered her hand but refused to let go completely.

"Arcaeus." He inclined his head. "My name is Arcaeus."

Arcaeus... It suited him. It suited the way he looked, and his name just seemed to purr and echo around in Arianna's head.

His gaze became more intense; it caused the butterflies in Arianna's stomach to take flight yet again. His gaze so intent on hers she almost forgot her hand was still clutched in his own. Arianna held her breath, the overwhelming sense that she could be swept away by the power of the emotions in his eyes almost sent her to her knees. They were so alive, and showed hurt and anguish, before those emotions became hidden away within the blink of an eye.

Already, the loss of connection caused Arianna's heart to constrict in her chest. It surprised her completely; her own neediness over a guy she hardly knew. Yet, deep down, she sensed she did know him, a feeling like déjà-vu.

He searched Arianna's face before he turned away. "You do not know me, then. Is my face not recognizable to you?"

Arianna watched as he paced, his large body somehow graceful. She took a calming breath, a little relieved to be away from those chocolate brown eyes.

"Should I know you?" Her heart screamed, *yes, you should!* but her head schemed with the archaeologist and decided this was definitely a dream and told her to get a damn grip.

"I will admit, Arcaeus, that I have the strangest sense that I know you or have met you before, but—well, I don't know. You can't be real." Arianna's simple yet honest reply caused Arcaeus to pace with what could only be called a childish stomp. He wasn't the only one frustrated with this situation. This was supposed to be a dream after all.

"I think I'm having a nervous breakdown," Arianna said out loud to no one in particular. She kept her eyes downcast as she started to fumble with the material of her chiton. She felt his gaze as it bored into her head, the air heavy with emotion.

"Listen, I've... Well, I really should be going." Arianna's voice was almost a squeak as she finally met his gaze. "It's been nice meeting you, Arcaeus."

Arianna smiled up at the warrior before she backed away and rubbed her sternum as she turned from him. The slight pain in her chest caused a frown to crease her forehead. Arianna lifted the skirt on her dress, her quickened pace taking her further away from a situation she just couldn't grasp, that she simply couldn't get her head around. Her walk soon turned to a jog, which became a run, her direction unknown but the need to get away overwhelming.

She didn't like the way this warrior had turned her own body against her, made her question her own feelings. And a dream male should not be as God damned sexy as he was. It just didn't make any sense.

Come to think about it, it was strange how she wasn't breathless after all this running. Her mind had drifted off to a world of its own. Arianna slowed down, and her hand found a home on an old oak tree. She leaned on it for support as she tried to free a twig from her sandal. It seemed even in dreams things seemed to get wedged where they weren't needed.

Arianna looked around, her eyes adjusting to the multitude of colours around her, and a realization that everything looked exactly the same struck her. She peered around the tree as she tried to look for a way out of this damn forest. She moved a step back, and in doing so, she felt her foot twist. In an attempt to put the other down, Arianna hit nothing but fresh air. Her arms wind milled, and she fell into a void, its blackness swallowing her screams.

Her last thought…

She never did get that second kiss!

Arianna's heart thundered against her ribcage as she sat bolt upright on the sofa, her ragged breathing unusually loud as she tried to regain control of her body. She pried open her fingers, white from the death grip she'd had on the plump cushion. Her loose-fitting t-shirt clung to her skin as another trickle of sweat ran a path down the back of her neck.

Her entire body ached. Her legs were sore, and her feet felt like small needles had pierced the base. All things she shouldn't be feeling, as she had never actually stepped foot into a forest. There was no way in hell she could believe that her dream was anything but that: a dream. Arianna leaned back on one hand as she reached up to push damp hair out of her face. The bird's nest on top of her head was going to need some serious tending to. She winced as she tugged on a lock, pulling out a small twig that had made its home within.

"You have got to be kidding me," she whispered to the empty room, her voice shaky and hoarse yet filled with disbelief

Arianna had clearly been more exhausted than she thought. She looked around the room, desperate for some sort of normalcy after one of the strangest dreams in her entire life, and that was saying something. For longer than she could remember, Arianna had always had strange dreams. It was why she was hooked on mythology. Her dreams had always been centred on Ancient Greece, along with the gods and goddesses that dominated their time.

Arianna swung her legs around, so her feet were flat on solid ground. Her toes flexed into the thick carpet as her gaze landed on the television and the static screen that was now being featured; the film she had put on long finished. Eager in her attempt to regain her sanity, Arianna stood and stretched her arms above her head as she mentally blamed her film choice and her hard week at work for her bizarre dreams and obviously overactive imagination. Arianna yawned long and loud and finished it up with a deep, heartfelt sigh.

"Arcaeus," she whispered as she fumbled and fidgeted with her shirt, pulling it down over her midriff. "Who the hell are you?"

Arianna stretched again. Sleeping on the sofa was definitely not a good idea, and her back was telling her about it now. She shuffled towards the bay window. Her hand clutched the edge of the thick material of the curtain and moved it to one side, the action giving her access to peer outside. It was a habit she had acquired from looking out for her dad when she was a child, waiting for him to come home from his night shift at work. The sky was still dark, made eerie by the fog that had crept through the trees, giving the landscape an almost magical appearance.

Arianna's jaw cracked loudly as she pulled off another monster yawn, her eyes flicking to the clock on the wall over the TV. Her mind, groggy at first, took in the time, as her brain clicked on and started to function. She realised that, even in the dark of the room with only the TV showing any light, she could see how early it was. She was definitely not a 5:30am sort of girl. She was barely a 7am kind of girl.

"Really," Arianna groaned, using the heel of her palms to rub her eyes. She felt mentally exhausted, but there was no way she would be able to get back to sleep. Her brain was now fully engaged. Typical, when she needed all the rest she could get.

Sleepily, she walked into the kitchen, bare feet slapping against the cool tiles as she beelined for the kettle and quickly turned it on. Arianna leaned back against the counter, her body still struggling to wake up, but her head soon drooped forward, and her eyes slid shut. Exhaustion took over for a moment, her mind drifting back to her bizarre dream.

The sound of the kettle clicking itself off was enough to bring Arianna back to semi-consciousness, enough that she was able to make a large mug of her favourite tea. Her hands gripped the mug tightly as she once again leaned back against the counter, sipping at the hot liquid until she felt almost awake enough to function and to do what needed to be done.

Mug in hand, she forced herself forward to the bathroom.

She stopped on her way past the bookshelf, grabbed one of her favourite novels, and threw it in her hand luggage, along with her purse and passport. All her bags packed and ready, the only thing left was to wake the hell up and make herself presentable for the trip.

5

Athens, Greece. The High Reign of Cimon.

Arcaeus fell forward onto his hands, his whole body shaking from the exertion of holding the connection. He took deep, slow breaths as he forced his heartrate to decrease and level out.

Gingerly, so as not to keel over, he stood, surprised when he got to his feet. He swayed a little as the dizziness hit him, so closed his eyes and rested his head against the wall. The cost of using his gift was great, but his need was so much greater.

Arcaeus hadn't offered his services to Apollo for nothing. He was given the gift of soul searching to connect with souls through dreams. This was his one and only chance of finding her.

Arcaeus started to feel a little more like himself as he perched on the end of his pallet. He pushed the heels of his hands into his eyes and tried to think back through the events of the past few months.

He had been completely shaken when he first saw her in the dream forest, his heart beating triple time as he looked upon the most beautiful face he had ever seen. His joy, though, had soon plummeted as he realised that she didn't recognise him. Even when Arcaeus had pressed his lips to hers and prayed she would remember, she had looked blankly into his face.

His hope, something he had relied heavily upon these past five years, was slowly dying and withering away.

He laid back on the bed, his body still humming with adrenaline—as well as being highly aroused. Arcaeus adjusted himself under his kilt. It had been an age since he had relieved himself. He just hadn't had the drive. But now... now, he had seen her, smelled her, tasted her, there was no going back. She was branded onto his very soul.

She may not have remembered him, but by the gods did he remember her. As brief as it had been, the feel of her body, her skin, and the touch of her lips, had set his body aflame. Yet he had been left frustrated. Frustrated that recognition eluded her, as well as being extremely uncomfortable in the kilt area.

Arcaeus took another deep breath, before his mind drifted back to when he had last seen her in the flesh. They used to meet in the gardens that surrounded the Temple of the Oracle in Delphi, a routine they never deviated from. She was always sat by the marble fountain in the heart of the gardens, always quiet and deep in thought as she sat and reflected. The gardens were open to all who wanted to visit the temple. Apollo liked that he could tempt people into his domain. Why she had chosen that god to serve, he never knew, and he had never asked. That never changed the fact that Arcaeus didn't trust him.

On that day he lost her, she had sat quietly, as always, when he approached her, her hands twisting and braiding a section of her hair—a habit for whenever she was nervous or just deep in thought.

Arcaeus had known something was wrong when he saw the ribbons tied to her wrists. Sacrificial ribbons. And the mark of one who had been chosen by their god.

She had stood and he'd simply taken her into his arms and kissed her head as he came to terms with the fact that the one woman he loved, his soul mate, was about to be taken away from him and sacrificed to a malicious god. The fact that all the gods did things for a reason, no matter how pathetic, made him angry.

She had looked him in the eye and told him she loved him, kissed him briefly on the lips—and then turned and walked away. Arcaeus had never, for one second, stopped loving her, and the grief of never seeing her again had driven him to Apollo, where he made a deal but always kept the reason for doing so to himself.

He relaxed his body as he willed his mind to rest. He had to plan carefully. He needed to find out where she was, and, most of all, he had to remind her of who he was and what they had meant to each other. The task was not an easy one, especially when he had to complete it before the gods found out. A god thwarted is never a happy god, but he refused to be beaten or admit defeat.

※

Greece, The Land of the Gods…

Arianna failed to hold back her smile of glee as she waited to exit the plane. The name sounded not just a little cheesy, but a lot cheesy. But it was true.

Arianna had always found Athens—Greece in general—so

enchanting, and to finally be there, to be given the opportunity to excavate some of the most famous sites in the world, was a dream come true.

But her dreams had been different of late. Maybe the dream she secretly craved to come true was the recurring one involving Arcaeus. She had spent the whole flight daydreaming of that warrior, thinking of all the things she would like to say and maybe—no, definitely—do to him. Arianna just couldn't get the man off her mind. It was like he was under her skin, pulsing through her bloodstream.

Arianna stepped off the plane and immediately tilted her head upwards. The bright sun and its warmth seeped into her travel weary bones. She hoisted her rucksack over her shoulder as she walked towards the passport control area. She refused to wait for Sonia, who had ditched her again. Her best friend had been too busy flirting with one of the stewards to notice her presence, something Arianna found difficult to do. In fact, talking to men in general had always been difficult for her, and she envied Sonia of that skill. At least Sonia's flight had been a pleasant one, but then again, she got all the luck. Arianna had been sat next to the one guy who kept the whole airplane awake with his snoring. She just couldn't believe it. And he sounded like a jet engine taking off. Constantly—for the *entire* four hours. She had never been a violent person, but if someone had given her a pillow, she wouldn't have hesitated to bloody well use it.

She stretched her legs and kept her pace slow, giving her tart of a best friend a chance to catch up and then bore her with her outstanding flirting skills and what she had accomplished in such a short amount of time. Arianna wished she could be as confident in the male department as her best mate.

She looked at her watch for what had to have been the

hundredth time. Sonia was seriously taking the proverbial piss. Arianna sighed as she realised it had been over an hour since the plane landed and she was still standing like a lemon as she waited. But that just seemed to be what happened on a regular occurrence lately. They had yet to collect their bags and catch a taxi to their apartment, and all Arianna wanted to do was grab some food and relax for the remainder of the day.

Why was it always her who observed from the outside? Arianna asked herself. Always her watching the exciting things happen but never being in the middle of it. It sometimes felt like she didn't belong, like she just didn't fit in.

"Damn it, Sonia, where the hell are you? Believe it or not, I do have a life," Arianna muttered to herself out loud, the sound rebounding off the empty corridor walls.

As if right on cue, Sonia appeared around the corner of the corridor with her hand on the steward's forearm, batting her eyelashes as he spoke. His head was bent towards her ear as they shared some intimate moment.

Arianna rolled her eyes. She knew this was one of Sonia's many and extensive techniques for landing a date. She plastered a smile on her face as they approached, then waited even as she noticed the same steward Sonia was plastered to give her the once over before grinning back at her best friend. He kissed Sonia's cheek before walking away, confident and with a typical male swagger. Arianna watched as her best friend walked towards her, covering the final few meters quickly. She suddenly felt her stomach twist and knot as she twigged on what had just happened, as she glimpsed the evil grin on Sonia's face.

"Well? Were you successful in your hunt?" Arianna said, far too sweetly. "And why the hell are you looking at me like that?" Sonia continued to grin, her look all-knowing as she waited for the penny to drop. After only a few seconds,

Arianna felt like Zeus himself had delivered a lightning bolt straight to her skull, and it suddenly dawned on her.

"NO! No way in hell, Sonia. You can stop what you are planning now because it isn't going to happen." Arianna folded her arms across her chest and just glared at Sonia.

She watched as a myriad of emotions flashed across Sonia's all too open face, before she blushed, then fidgeted. Her next words shot Arianna's anxiety skyward.

"Yes, Anya, I was very successful. Would you expect anything less from me?" Sonia shot her a self-satisfied grin, then waved a napkin in Arianna's face. A blur of black ink signalled the location of the steward's number as the tissue flew across her vision.

"I have his number and his current address here, but…" Sonia threw on her innocent look and batted her eyelashes as she brought her hands up to her chest in a mock praying action, "I have a small problem, which you *need* to help me with."

Silence followed this statement as the two best friends just looked at each other, but deep down, Arianna already knew what was about to happen.

"Go on, Sonia, say it."

Sonia took an overexaggerated breath before she began her full assault explanation, and, of course, her evil master plan.

"Well, he has this friend, who is just as hot as Steven, and he doesn't want to leave him on his own. So… when he saw you, he thought it would be nice for us all to, well, you know —to double date." Sonia shot her last sentence out in a rush, seeming somehow in the belief that the faster she said it, the better it would sound. She changed her hand luggage over to her other shoulder before she passed Arianna, head held high, and moved towards passport control, her feet quickly eating up the distance.

"*What?*" Arianna let out a screech so loud it caused the dozing Greek security guard to eye them both suspiciously. "And what—you told him yes, without even asking me first?"

Arianna grabbed her hand luggage and rushed to catch up with her best friend, her mouth opening and closing like a goldfish. She was still in shock from the news she'd just been delivered.

"Sonia," Arianna whispered angrily as they waited side by side in the queue, her hands clenching tightly, causing her fingernails to dig into her palms. "I am not, I repeat, NOT, double dating with you. Not again, Sonia," Arianna spat out through clenched teeth.

Sonia answered with a sweet smile and a small nod, the only sign Arianna had been listened to at all. The subject was definitely not dropped, or over, as far as she was concerned.

Sonia breezed through passport control and marched off to find her bag. A slightly dumbstruck Arianna was left to trail behind, and the mumbled curses that came from her lips had the other travellers eyeing her warily.

Arianna felt her stomach drop as they exited the airport and headed to the taxi station. Why couldn't her friend just leave her be, leave her to be miserable and single, but free from getting hurt? She just knew, deep down, this date was going to be a disaster.

6

"Why did I agree to this, Anya? Look at my nails!"

Arianna chuckled as said nails were wafted in front of her face while they walked into what was going to be their apartment for the next three months.

The apartment had a nice compact and airy plan, which also came with a fabulous view of the city. The spectacular expanse of the ocean could be seen from the balcony in Arianna's bedroom. They were lucky there was a cleaner and a pool housed within the complex, as well as a small shop just around the corner.

"I don't know why you're moaning, Sonia. You knew full well what we were going to be doing when you signed up for it." Arianna smiled to herself. She didn't feel mean in the slightest, not after all the stunts Sonia had pulled on her. Arianna loved her best friend very much, but dear God above, she could moan. Sonia was definitely what you would call a girly girl. A small fact Arianna was secretly jealous of. Men loved Sonia; they never seemed to look twice at Arianna.

"But my nails... Just look!" Arianna watched as Sonia rushed past her, then doubled back to look in the mirror hanging in the lounge area.

"Oh my God, is that dirt on my nose? Anya, I have dirt on my damn nose!" Her voice just seemed to go higher and higher in pitch, which, in turn, made Arianna snort, then giggle. Sonia's answering glare caused Arianna to throw her hand over her mouth to stop the snort that wanted to be released

"Fine, laugh all you like, Anya." Sonia's smile, far too sweet in its appearance to be a good sign, worried Arianna almost immediately. "But we do have tonight's fabulous double date to look forward to."

Arianna dropped her hand and hung her head. She had totally forgotten about the dreaded experience to come. Her day had been wonderful, just like the others had been since their arrival a few weeks back. She had been totally engrossed in her work. If only she had thought about pulling a sicky. She knew she was frowning hard as she walked past her best mate, face averted in an attempt to hide her features.

"Anya, I know that look." Arianna winced and cursed quietly. Sonia had eyes like a hawk. She noticed everything.

"You are not getting out of this. You promised." Sonia produced a childish stomp to emphasize her words.

Arianna sighed as she started to walk to her room. She threw an answer over her shoulder. "Sonia, I agreed, so I will do it, okay? Just don't expect me to have a good time."

She shut her bedroom door and fingered the small pendant around her neck: Arianna's good luck charm. It had been around her neck since she was nine years old, and she always found caressing the small, round coin soothing. She had found it on holiday with her parents. The small pendant had washed up on the beach, shining like a beacon in the water. She had been mesmerised by it.

It was a dull silver, sort of like pewter, but with symbols that went into a spiral pattern. It was only after she finished her studies and knew more of the ancient cultures that she recognised it as Ancient Greek. Now Arianna's fingers lovingly stroked the etching as the words echoed through her mind.

Blessed, Aphrodite, here my call. May the cool sea water cleanse my soul in honour of you, may the crisp air banish my sins, may the earth centre my being, and may fire ignite my passions. Let my heart lead me to what is true. With your blessing, I seek my soul, my heart, my love.

Internally, Arianna sighed. No matter how beautiful the words might be, they were just that: words. Nothing more, nothing less. She let the pendant drop back onto her chest as she headed for the bathroom. A long, hot shower was definitely needed if she was to face this disaster of a date.

Steam bellowed out from behind Arianna as she stepped back into her room, rubbing her damn hair with a towel vigorously before she sat at the dressing table, another towel still wrapped tight around her torso. Arianna picked up her favourite hairbrush and held it in a loose grip. She slowly swept it down her long locks to free the knots, the bristles tugging gently as she stared into the mirror.

The deep green of her irises stared back at her, their reflection seeming to pop with hints of gold flecked throughout them. Tilting her head, Arianna leaned forward, her face almost hitting the glass as she became mesmerized by the colours that seemed to swirl and pulse from the reflection of her own eyes. Her gaze began to lose focus slightly, fog quickly giving way to images that appeared out of nowhere. They played across the surface of the mirror in what could only be described as a vision, like she was watching a fuzzy video.

A woman stood with her back to Arianna, her hair a riot

of curls that fell all the way down her back. She wore a chiffon dress of pale green that caressed her body, showcasing her curves to the full. She was stunning, so much so Arianna suddenly felt envious. Slowly, the woman turned, and her features came into view. Arianna felt her mouth loosen in shock. The woman in the mirror was Arianna! The same, yet somehow... different.

Arianna's gaze became drawn to the pendant around her mirror-self's neck and the strange black ribbons around her wrists.

She smiled at Arianna, as if she knew she was being watched. Arianna's body started to shake as her mirror image mouthed, "Go... Aphrodite."

The woman's face turned serious, and her frown deepened as Arianna's own body temperature plummeted. The vision started to fade, disappearing in a fog of red mist.

"Protect him, save him. Save his soul." The voice, more like a whisper, flowed through Arianna's mind.

Arianna blinked, the simple movement easily breaking whatever spell had been weaved. The vision instantly disappeared, leaving Arianna once again faced with her own normal reflection, her eyes just their normal green with no sign of the gold, no hint of the swirling or pulsing. Only her racing heart belied the fact that something strange had happened.

"What the hell was that?" she whispered, and her hands shook as she pushed back from the dressing table. Arianna's eyes were still locked on the mirror as she stumbled back onto the bed. Her arse hit the sheets so hard she bounced on the soft mattress.

Arianna repeated to herself, as her heartrate continued to go off on a gallop, "What the fuck was that?"

She took slow, deep breaths, her hands fisting the bed linens, clenching and releasing over and over. After what felt like an age, Arianna stopped. She released the soft material from her tight grip and looked down at her fingers, which had unconsciously twisted in the soft fabric of the dress she was supposed to be wearing for the evening. In an attempt to calm her heart and nerves, she smoothed the material down, her hand pressed flat on the silk as she took long, deep breaths again.

"Arianna, are you ready yet? We have to be there in an hour." The excited sound of Sonia's voice penetrated through the thick fog that surrounded Arianna's dazed mind, and the towel dropped from her body as she jumped to get ready.

She made a grab for her underwear and shouted a reply. "Nearly, Sonia. Just doing my hair."

Arianna turned back to the mirror, her hair a riot of curls, as it always was when it got wet. She decided to go for the natural look. She picked up a bottle of macadamia oil, her one and only girly vice, before squirting the oil onto her palm. She rubbed her hands together then quickly smoothed the liquid through her loose, bouncy curls. Faced with her reflection, Arianna grabbed some pins from her travel vanity case and inserted them randomly into the hair now pinned loosely to the top of her head. She collected a dark black eyeliner pencil and her favourite mascara, then quickly completed her eyes, before finishing off the look with pale pink lip-gloss.

Arianna slipped into the light blue dress, the feel of it soft against her skin as she walked over to the full-length mirror. Her eyes widened a little as she took in her reflection. Wow! Arianna twisted and turned, surprised at how a few weeks in the sun and some good old-fashioned archaeology could make her look and feel attractive for once.

She made some last-minute checks. Did she have everything; purse, phone? After one last look in the mirror, she smiled and left her room. The loud, overexcited voice of

Sonia filled the apartment as a clear knock was heard at the front door.

*O*h *my God, could this guy be any more boring?* That simple mantra continuously repeated its way around Arianna's mind as she sat and pretended to enjoy the company of… What was his name again? Oh yeah, Andrew.

Arianna thought he was alright looking, but for the last hour he had droned on and on about himself; where he had been, the places he had seen, the things he had done.

So, because she was such a sweet and kind person, she did the nicest thing a good friend could do: she smiled sweetly and nodded in response to his questions—when he asked them. She even laughed at his jokes. Yet her mind, as usual, kept wandering to *him*, to Arcaeus. All she could focus on was how his hair was silky, brown and long, not short and blonde like Andrew's. How his eyes, which held warmth and tenderness, were chocolate brown, not the icy blue of Andrew's. And not for the life of her could she forget the perfection that was Arcaeus's body; just like many of the statues dotted around Greece herself, though none as perfect as him. Personally, she didn't even want to picture what Andrew looked like with no clothes on. She felt herself shudder at the thought, unfortunately drawing Andrews's attention.

"So, Anya… that's a different name. Is it short for anything?" Why did she feel as though he looked down his nose at her? Typical male; arrogant, always quick to judge a book by its cover. She watched as he sipped from his large glass of wine.

"Yes, it's short for Arianna. It's European." She smiled and tried to act sincere.

"Mmm, yes. Nice. Have you visited a lot of Europe, Anya? Other than Greece, that is." He said her name with a slight sneer. "I find the different cultures wonderfully diverse, and the women are so much…"

Arianna eyes widened. Surely, he wasn't… Andrew continued to drone on, unaware of the direction he was about to take the conversation, and the consequences of stepping over that particular line. Her eyes narrowed as he gestured to Stephen and Sonia.

"Yes, the women in Europe certainly know how to appeal to the men. Now, don't take this the wrong way, Anya." Oh, dear God, he'd gone there. She clenched her fists under the table, her mind screaming what an arrogant prick he was.

He continued with his little speech, unaware of the icy glare that was now being shot in his direction. "You see, European women just know how to lure a man; their figures are just that little bit slenderer!"

Oh my God, he did. The prick went there.

"Oh? Okay." Arianna grinned in response, looking directly into his face. "So, Andrew, are you, in a sort of strange way, informing me that I'm fat?" Arianna said this with extra sweetness, clipping the end of the question. She wondered if the arsehole had any idea what he had just done. Inside, she was desperate to slap that stupid, conceited smile off his face.

"What? No, Anya, I would never be so… um…" He failed to meet her gaze as his throat and cheeks started to turn a deep crimson, as beads of sweat broke out on his brow. He never replied, just sat and coughed in an attempt to clear his throat. Arianna had had enough of this git and his superior opinion on women, and what he thought a woman should look and dress like. She stood up and grabbed her purse, clasping it tightly in her fist.

"Well, Andrew, thank you so much for telling me my

faults in your oh so perfect way. May I just remind you of the fact that I am the more qualified person here. What's your job again? Oh yes, a male trolley dolly, who most people assume is gay." Arianna grabbed her glass of white wine, careful not to spill anything on her dress—and launched the contents straight into his face. Unable to help herself, Arianna grinned and watched as he spluttered and tried to grab a napkin.

"I'm sure you can find plenty of European women here for your personal enjoyment. Oh, and before I go... your fly's been undone all evening, and you have some of your lunch in your teeth. Try looking in the mirror before judging others." Arianna pushed her chair further back and stood away from the table. She mouthed a goodbye to Sonia, whose face was a picture of shock as she looked from Andrew to Arianna.

In a desperate bid to leave, Arianna raced outside as fast as her three-inch heels could carry her. She needed some fresh air and solitude. Arianna let her feet take her away from the restaurant and the bustle of people, to the peace and quiet of the ruins and temples. Not for the first time in her life, and probably not the last time either, Arianna repeated an old mantra.

"Bastard bloody men!"

7

Arianna wandered through the ruins that were dotted around the site in Peiraias. Her hands lightly trailed over the fallen marble blocks as she meandered along a short path, no real destination in mind, and tried to calm herself down. Men were such arseholes! Arianna was still in total shock that the git had the nerve to make out she wasn't woman enough, that she didn't know how to attract men, that, in short, she was fat. Really! Why do men do that? Of course, she could attract men. She just chose not to.

"Seriously!" She gave an unladylike snort and shook her head. "Am I really that repulsive?"

Arianna's voice broke; the echo of her shattered confidence floating over the field of debris and out into the moonlit night. She let her emotions run free, and her tears fell continuously as she picked her way through the ruins.

She clutched her purse to her chest as if her life depended on it. It was almost as though, if she let go of the purse, she would lose herself.

Her meanderings soon became stumbles, her sandaled feet hitting a block of stones. She cried out, and all the pain and hurt she had been dealt over the years culminated in tears of anguish and rejection. Arianna kept her head cast downward as her tears splattered against her cheeks, before rolling down her chin and neck. She just didn't care anymore.

So lost in her own emotions, the beauty and tranquillity that surrounded her was forgotten, until only the pain and hurt remained; memories of those few times she had let herself feel love. Arianna snorted. Love didn't exist. It was purely a myth, just like the gods and goddesses she daydreamed about. It was a tool, an excuse to lie to someone, use them and then hurt them.

After what felt like hours, but was in fact only one at the most, Arianna slumped down onto some steps and wrapped her arms around her knees. She kicked off her sandals and flexed and wiggled the toes that were slightly swollen from their contact with the marble, attempting to calm the raging sobs that wracked her whole body, her breaths hiccupping on every exhale.

"Why me? Why does this happen every time?" Arianna whispered the question out into the night, but she knew full well that she wouldn't receive a response. The silence was only broken now and again by the sound of a cricket and a lonely cat also looking for solace. Arianna's mind felt like an old-fashioned record player that played over and over on repeat. Deep down inside her, Arianna felt an overwhelming sense of… emptiness? A gut feeling told her that something, or someone, was missing from her life. She felt like a hole had been vacant throughout her years but had quietly gone unnoticed. Until now, she hadn't even realised she wasn't complete.

Arcaeus, a warrior from her imagination... In the brief moments they had shared, he seemed to have filled that void, almost as if they belonged together, which was silly when she considered that he didn't exist other than in her dreams. Clearly, it had taken her subconscious, well aware of that emptiness, to scream at her for her to notice that missing piece.

Very slowly, Arianna managed to calm the sobs. Her breathing smoothed out and the tears stopped falling, but their existence was still noticeable across her cheeks. Using the heel of her palm, she smudged the tear tracks from her cheeks and looked up to take in her location. Her butt was firmly planted on the stone steps that lead up to the main temple in Peiraias, Temple to Hera, Zeus and Aphrodite. Arianna looked around, her breathing returned to normal, as her hands dug inside her overly large purse in search of some tissues.

Mid-search, the hairs on the back of her neck rose and caused a shiver to shoot down her spine. Her body froze as she heard the faint echo of something being dropped onto the floor of the ruined structure behind her. Slowly, Arianna turned her head and peered into the shadowed entrance. Her eyes struggled to adjust to the darkness that not even the lamps seemed to be able to penetrate.

"Hello? Is anyone there?" Arianna's voice echoed around the ruins, the sound faint and lost.

She stood in a deliberate move laced with caution, her gaze locked on the large, looming entrance as she turned and faced the opening of what she could now confirm and recognise as the remains of a temple. Its structure huge and domineering, its size was masked in both shadow and pure moonlight.

The doorway, even in its ruined state, stood proud and beautifully ornate. The white marble, although cast in shadow, was just as wondrous. The columns that framed each side were complete with flowing golden veins that sparkled in even the smallest amount of light. Carved reliefs of nymphs, gods and mortals decorated the walls, seeming like they had only been created yesterday.

Arianna smiled, her fear soon forgotten as she brushed her fingers across the raised marble, drawing them over beasts and humans, their beauty overwhelming in their simplicity. She rested her hand on one of the carvings, as if using it for courage, and again beseeched the dark.

"Hello?" Her voice, this time higher in pitch, was more than a little shaky. The squeak echoed throughout the structure. Arianna moved her hand from the carving and placed it on the wall, the chill of the stone instantly seeping into her palm. Goosebumps shot up her arm and travelled down her body. She failed to hold back a shudder, almost as if someone had walked over her grave. She took a deep, long breath, gathered her courage, and prepared herself for anything she might encounter. Clutching her purse tightly, Arianna stepped through the shadowed doorway.

She held one hand out in front of her, feeling her way through the darkness. She moved quickly through the structure and stepped out of the shadows into the main atrium. The size, at first, took her by surprise, and then she was struck dumb at the beauty presented to her.

"Oh!" she breathed.

Moonlight filtered through the broken ceiling, creating beams of almost white light, her gaze undecided on where to look first as the beam directed on what used to be the main altar to Zeus. His tall, muscular frame dominated the room, and even though the main bulk of the statue was damaged, it had lost none of its majesty. It was spectacular to behold. It was easy to see why he had been seen as the king of gods.

Arianna smiled as she moved past Zeus. Her fear now

gone, she was more than eager to explore more of the cavernous temple. She peeked to the left and was able to see a recess as the moonlight filtered through the breaks in the ceiling. It highlighted the cracked and crumbling statue of Hera, mother of the gods and wife to Zeus. Arianna stopped briefly to stare at its splendour, a little sad that the head of the statue was missing.

She continued onwards, her eyes drinking everything in. The archaeologist in her moved to the forefront, seeking out the knowledge hidden in these ruins, the drama and pain from earlier locked away for now. Arianna wished she had her notebook with her, and her camera and brushes. She didn't think she would ever again get the chance to have unrestricted access to this temple, and honestly, she was surprised there were no security ropes to keep people away. She didn't doubt for a second that this temple would be swarming with tourists during the day. A turn to the right, and Arianna walked towards the opposite alcove from Hera, as though some unseen force pulled her in that direction and needed her to see what resided in the shadows.

A single statue stood alone, the marble clean and perfect. The gold veins sparkled in the light, as if covered in glitter. Arianna's gaze was pulled up, and like a puppet on a string, it lifted higher and higher. The statue was that of a woman, nearly complete, unlike the others. It stood well over twelve feet in height. Her body was in a relaxed pose, her face serene as a secret smile played across her lips while she looked towards the other deities. Her pose was one of protection and love.

"Aphrodite!" Her name escaped Arianna's lips in a revenant whisper as she approached, moving toward the statue. Her left hand reached out. For some unknown reason, she felt she needed to touch the goddess's statue, needed to feel the marble beneath her palm. Her right hand reached up and stroked the pendant at her throat as she stared in awe up at the goddess.

The earlier vision replayed over and over inside of her head as her gaze travelled over the stunning marble form. She reached out, this time with both hands, and placed her palms flat against the marble. She expected it to be cool, but instead, her skin met with warmth. The heat sent tingles up her arms and across her skin. The archaeologist inside Arianna was quick to study the detail in the craftsmanship and the outstanding beauty that was before her. Her own heart and soul wished in earnest for the gods to be real.

She spoke out loud, the sound of her voice alien in the serene and silent surroundings. "Why are you suddenly so important in my life? Why does everything point to you when you are just a simple statue?"

Arianna shook her head and continued with her rambling, not in the slightest bit bothered who saw her or if anyone heard her talking to herself. "Why, when you are not real? Gods and goddesses don't exist. Is it only in my dreams that you walk alongside mortals?"

Arianna laughed at her own stupidity. She didn't doubt she looked foolish talking to a statue. "You're being silly now, Anya. You've daydreamed far too much, and you know those dreams will never come true because, and I stress, Anya," she berated herself, her tone becoming angrier, more with herself than anything else, "gods and," she gazed again up at Aphrodite's face, "goddesses do not exist!"

At Arianna's open denial of belief, a strong gust of wind coursed its way through the temple, not cool but warm and inviting. It swirled around her body, as if in protection. It brought with it the scent of blooming narcissus flowers. The fragrance reminded Arianna of her dreams and of the brown-eyed warrior who haunted them and her every waking hour.

Arianna smiled to herself and closed her eyes. She took the opportunity to enjoy the strange, almost magical, phenomenon, and for once she let the dreamer inside come out, the scientist inside forgotten.

She moved slowly, the heavy purse slipping from her fingers. The loud thud of it hitting the floor echoed throughout the empty temple.

Her eyes closed tight, the wind swirled around her dress and caressed her bare shoulders as though offering an invitation, an invitation to dance and move.

She turned slowly and moved away from the immense marble figure. Allowing her body to flow with the wind, she twirled and twisted. Her mind somehow conjured soft, lilting music that filtered into the building. It blended with the wind, its location a magical, welcome mystery.

Arianna let her body go. She felt freer than she had ever before, and she wanted, for once, to enjoy something not tainted by real life, something that could only happen in a world where gods and goddesses existed.

With her arms held above her head, Arianna moved in a slow rhythm, and she smiled with joy, overcome by a lightness she never knew possible, a freedom of body and mind that was so exquisite, she was unable to stop the silent, happy tears that started to fall down her cheeks. Arianna closed her eyes, lost as she revelled in the dance before the gods.

In the heat of the moment and under the spell of the dance, words started to pour from Arianna's lips. They spilled out like a fountain of radiant water. A blessing—no, *the* blessing—from the pendant securely fastened around her neck. The words were spoken from her heart, flowing out, their echo loud and clear throughout the temple.

"*Blessed Aphrodite,*" Arianna called out, her voice breathless from the dance yet still loud and confident. *"Hear my call. May the cool sea water cleanse my soul in honour of you, may the crisp air banish my sins in honour of you, may the earth centre my being in honour of you, and may fire ignite my passions in honour of you. Let my heart lead me to what is true. With your blessing, I seek my soul, my heart, my love. Blessed be thy goddess, Aphrodite."*

Arianna fell to her knees as she ended the blessing, her chest heaving from the exertion. She opened her eyes to look up at the statue of the goddess. She blinked, trying to focus as her eyes filled with tears. The music had vanished, along with the wind. The magic of the night slowly vanished as well, almost as if it had never been.

She took a deep breath and slowly got to her feet, her body unsteady and her mind a little groggy. She moved towards the altar and bent down to scoop up her purse from the floor. Her head felt dizzy as she moved to straighten and put out her hand to steady herself on the nearest column. She attempted to regain her composure.

"God this seems to be happening to me more and more lately, and I haven't even had a drink." She stumbled past the statue; her hands placed on the walls in an effort to help with her balance as she made her way through the beautiful temple.

Strange, Arianna thought to herself, *it doesn't look like a ruin.* Arianna gazed around, much like a child in a toy shop, wanting to take every detail in.

"It definitely didn't look like this when I walked in." Everything now seemed new, brand new, and where the hell did those sconces come from?

A small chuckle from behind made Arianna jump. She stopped, ready to turn, her purse clutched tight in her hand, ready to strike out if needed. In her attempt, Arianna felt a tug and found she was unable to turn as something, or someone, had a firm hold of her arm. She tugged and pulled in an attempt to free herself, but in the same instance, her balance was lost.

Arianna reached out to grab something, but her hands closed around fresh air as she tumbled down the few steps that led the way out of the rear of the temple.

A flash of red material and blonde hair, followed by a voice, accompanied her as she took the tumble. Arianna's head connected with the hard ground. Before her mind lost all thought and drifted into oblivion, a stranger's voice could be heard, a mere whisper into her ear.

"I hear you, Arianna Jane. Your plea I answer. Your heart and soul are true. Be at ease, my priestess. All will happen as it should."

"The Goddess and her Companion"

"My lady, was that really necessary? Did you have to push her down the stairs?" Meton asked from his perch on the wall outside of the temple. He looked down at the unconscious form of Arianna and turned his feathered head, his gaze now fixed upon the goddess Aphrodite.

"I didn't push her, Meton. She slipped on the step. Anyway, that's not the point. She would have noticed that things were..." she waved a delicate hand about as only goddesses do and indicated to the not so ruined temple and surrounding buildings, "not as she thought," Aphrodite finished. She took a breath before she continued to explain her plan. "She isn't stupid, and without Arcaeus here, I didn't really want her knowing that I'd been a naughty goddess and brought her back in time. The shock of that alone would be a bit much, even for one as clever as Arianna."

Meton shifted his claws on the marble and continued to stare blankly at Aphrodite.

"Oh, stop it, Meton," she snapped, but with no real heat in her words. "She will handle the time travel situation better if she is in the presence of her soul mate."

Aphrodite walked down the stairs and paused. Bending down, she checked on Arianna, gently brushing the hair from the fallen woman's face.

"She may not remember him from her previous life, but her soul knows him. They belong together." Aphrodite's lips spread into a sweet, charming smile, and she tilted her head to look at her companion. Meton had always been there and always told her his honest opinion. For an eagle, he was extremely romantic.

"Why, my lady, I was under the impression you never meddled in the lives of mortals. Especially not across time."

"Meton." Her voice turned serious as she leaned against the wall, next to where the eagle sat. "An injustice was done many years ago. I intend to right that wrong. Look at her. Do you recognize her?"

She turned and met the eagle's gaze as her hand gently slid across the feathers on his back. He broke the stare of the goddess and let his eyes wander, taking in the mortal who lay sprawled at the bottom of the stairs to the temple.

"That I do, my lady. I believe she belonged to Apollo. That is, in her past life. If I remember correctly, he demanded her sacrifice." Aphrodite nodded in agreement, also gazing down at Arianna, her eyes soft and filled with love. "Correct, Meton, but I will leave it at that for now. No need to dwell on things that are not important to the moment."

The unlikely duo stood in silence, both lost in their own thoughts as the early morning birdsong filled the air, the slow, steady breathing of the unconscious Arianna the only other sound. Meton looked again at his mistress and watched as she released a long, weary sigh. "My lady, you are troubled?"

"You didn't hear her plea, Meton." Aphrodite's eyes filled with tears. "Her heart and soul cried out to me. I couldn't ignore that. This mortal deserves my help, and she wears the pendant that identifies her as my priestess."

Aphrodite frowned, and her hand stilled on the eagle's head as she became lost in thought for a few seconds before shaking her head.

"Plus," she said with a grin, standing upright and adjusting her chiton, "the Goddess of Love demands a happy ending. Now, let us be off. I have made sure she will not wake for a while."

"My lady, she will be unprotected. "Surely, you cannot leave her here." The worry in Meton's voice made Aphrodite smile. Her companion was already fond of her new priestess. She raised an eyebrow as he continued, "Won't she be confused and scared, especially at not being able to understand anyone? I don't think she speaks Ancient Greek."

"Worry not, my friend. All will be well and will work out according to my plan, but first... fate must take a hand, and I must allow events to take their course. As much as I wish it to be different, Meton, it is desperately important." The goddess smiled affectionately. "With regards to her understanding the language, she is, in her soul, an Ancient Greek priestess. It may take a short while, but she will remember. Our Arianna will adapt. Of that I am certain."

The goddess leaned down to Arianna once again and placed a small kiss on her forehead, the injury that had knocked her unconscious vanishing at her gentle touch, before she whispered, "Rest well, Arianna. Save your strength. Your destiny awaits."

Aphrodite grinned as she straightened to her full height and walked into the temple, the bright flare of light the only sign of her visit—that, and the tiny speck of a golden eagle circling in the sky, keeping watch over the priestess, ready to assist should he be needed.

8

She could hear voices, and they weren't quiet. They were loud and unruly. Arianna wanted to sit up and throw her pillow at them, but she just knew her head couldn't take it. She felt like she had a serious hangover, and her eyes hadn't even opened yet.

How much had she drunk last night?

And why the hell was she so uncomfortable? Had she fallen asleep on the hard, leather couch again? She steeled herself for what she knew was going to be the mother of all migraines and opened her eyes, instantly flinching as the bright, golden sunlight hit her retinas.

"Holy shit! Someone turn out the lights." She rolled over onto her stomach and buried her head under her arms. She felt sick as a dog and so damn groggy, and she just couldn't remember what had happened last night.

The voices became louder, the sound of their feet crunching upon the grass. *Whoa! Grass?* Arianna, her head still sheltered beneath her arms, opened her eyes to narrow slits. The muted light made it easier to focus on what she currently lying on.

Grass, luscious green grass, complete with daisies. She felt confused and could tell she had a huge frown spread across her forehead. Her mother had always said she looked her worse when she frowned; she had described her as a half-breed Klingon from *Star Trek*.

She placed her palms flat upon the grass and pushed up, not surprised when her head swam, and her vision went blurry. Arianna moved just enough so she was able to sit on her arse and face toward the voices that had now stopped. But she knew the owners were close by. Arianna finally opened her eyes and squinted against the daylight, then opened them wider as her eyes adjusted to the brightness.

The temple looked exquisite in the daylight, so clean and sharp, the beauty so breath-taking it actually stilled her brain. Then Arianna remembered... the date, the disaster that was the date, and her lonesome foray into the ruins. Oh, and she could never forget her daft dance and blessing to Aphrodite.

Arianna laughed to herself as she thought about the dance. She must have drunk more than she thought to have done that and then go arse over tit down the stairs. She reached up to rub her head, finding a small lump present just above her left eye. It was tender to touch.

"Ouch, that hurts. That's it, Anya, no more booze for you —or blind dates, for that matter."

As if suddenly aware, Arianna looked up and into the worried faces of two men dressed in plain white chitons that reached their knees. They continuously threw her concerned looks. Arianna tried to get to her feet gracefully, her purse and sandals left on the grass where she had lay.

"Hello, sorry to disturb you but you could you point me in the direction of the nearest taxi?"

Arianna's simple question was met by blank stares, unnerving blank stares. She smiled her sweetest, friendliest smile that she reserved for prospective sponsors for the museum and spoke some of the only Greek words she knew.

"Geiá sou *(hello there)*." Arianna hoped she had the pronunciation right; she hoped she had the *language* right. English was the language she spoke best, and she stuck to it. She had always been terrible in her French classes at school, so much so she had made her teacher wince.

Holding her smile, she waited for a response. Instead, all she received was icy glares from the men as they looked her up and down. They seemed awfully focused upon her state of dress, and something deep down in her stomach turned over. She had a bad feeling about this.

After just a second, Arianna decided her best bet was to get up and leave now. She nodded, smiled, and backed away slowly, before she turned and faced the temple once again. Now fully functioning on all cylinders, Arianna noticed the difference; not just that the temple looked better in sunlight but that the temple was now whole, as in brand new. The columns were all complete and sparkled in the sunlight, the reliefs and carvings stood out more prominent and begged to be touched, and the glint of gold shone everywhere.

"What the hell," Arianna whispered to herself. This was not how the temple had looked last night. Her spectators forgotten, Arianna could only stare, her mind in a constant summersault.

This could not be real. She just couldn't fathom how in the hell a rundown ancient temple could appear as new as the day it was finished. Her thoughts so focused on the spectacle in front of her, she didn't see her new guests until they had a firm grip on both of her elbows.

Arianna looked to both sides and was met with the hard stares of two Greek soldiers, both decked out to the nines in full armour, including sharp-looking swords.

Confusion mounted as Arianna tried to tug herself free,

only to be restrained tighter. Their cold voices now penetrated through the confused haze of her brain. She had absolutely no idea what they were saying, but she had a bloody good idea that it wasn't good for her. Arianna looked towards the gentlemen that had been present when she had awoken, only to be met by ugly sneers and victorious grins.

"Excuse me, I suggest you get your sweaty man paws off me before I start to scream."

Nothing. Not even an acknowledgement that she had spoken. Arianna was led away, her hands still clenched into fists, a tight frown creasing her forehead.

Shit! What in the hell had she gotten herself into this time? Arianna hoped this was just a seriously fucked up dream and that she would wake up some time soon with that hangover she had originally dreaded.

Arcaeus scanned the countryside. Being a warrior of Greece, he was always on guard; not that anything would happen here. This had been his home all his life. Except for his training, he had never really left. Too many memories held him in a tight grip.

Smiling a little, he let his horse have the rein. He was in no hurry. This was his day off, the one day he could relax and visit the place that brought him some sort of peace. Not only had he lost his love five years ago, but he had lost the one person he had come to rely on for her wisdom and support.

His mother's grave stood not far from the main temple of Aphrodite, as well as those that belonged to Zeus and Hera. She had passed away not long after his father. The grief of a broken heart had been too much for her to take, and he could fully understand that.

For his heart was still in two, because whilst hope had

bloomed after locating his soul mate, he felt he had lost her again. After trying continuously for over a week, he hadn't been able to make the connection again, almost like she had vanished from the face of the earth.

He had been so close, but she still had not known him, and he couldn't understand why. Surely, she should have recognised him. He was hers after all. They were a pair. That was always what he had been taught to believe.

Arcaeus stopped his horse by the gate to the cemetery and petted his loyal friend. Named after one of the immortal stallions to the gods, this horse was surprisingly stuck up.

"I won't be long, Balios." He patted the steed's neck before heading through the wooden gate to what he knew would be the most well-kept and beautiful grave there, a small, simple bouquet of wildflowers gently clasped in his palm.

Its simplicity was the key to its beauty. A single statue stood alone, the white and black marble mix glittering in the sun as Arcaeus approached. It depicted his mother, standing with one hand on her chest, the other holding a single rose. A fitting memorial for the woman who had given him so much.

He knelt in front of the statue and closed his eyes, sending a silent prayer to the gods, specifically Hades. He prayed his mother was happy and worry free, finally at peace with his father in the Fields of Elyssia.

Arcaeus opened his eyes and took slow, deep breaths. He kissed his fingertips before placing them on the statue's feet. His heartrate was slow and steady as he got to his feet, his face a blank mask that showed no emotion. A trait he was well known for.

He took a step away from the statue and turned to leave, but something caught his eye. A golden eagle was sat on the boundary wall that surrounded the temple of the gods. The elegant bird gazed back at the warrior; its eyes filled with a knowing wisdom. Arcaeus stepped closer, and the golden feathers seemed to ripple, like the surface of a pool when a stone was dropped into it.

The bird quickly seemed to get bored with the warrior and turned its head to stare at something beyond the wall. With curiosity eating at him, Arcaeus slowly moved in the direction the eagle was staring, trying his hardest not to startle the bird, for to be in its presence was surely a sign from the gods that his prayers and service had brought him favour.

He neared the wall, its height only just reaching his waist, and spied a shoe, a small, dainty shoe, one he was sure belonged to a female. He leaned over the wall a little more, his large hands braced against the stone, and wondered if the owner was still present.

When he found no sign of her, Arcaeus vaulted over the wall, concerned about the safety for the unknown woman. He crouched down next to the sandal and easily found its mate, before standing to his full height and looking around him. There was no sign of anyone, not even the priests that worked at the temple daily. He looked down again at the sandals clutched within his grasp, a gut feeling telling him these sandals, as mundane as they looked, were crucially important to him and his future.

Arcaeus turned back to the wall, ready to be off. He could hear Balios by the gate, pawing at the ground, eager to be on the move.

With sure-footed steps, he moved towards the wall. Something crunched beneath his shoe as it connected with a foreign object forgotten on the ground.

He looked down at the grass, and there, in the bed of green leaves, was an unusual silver bag. It glittered like a gem, but when he bent to touch and pick the item up, it felt soft in his large hand. Arcaeus frowned as he placed the sandals on the wall and took the bag in both hands, gently turning it this way and that. He enjoyed the shimmer of light as he tilted it into the sun's rays. Lost in the sparkle, Arcaeus had forgotten about his feathered friend, but its loud squawk and the rustle of feathers reminded Arcaeus of its presence.

The great bird, as if bored with the goings on with a simple mortal man, lifted its huge head, its gaze ancient and knowledgeable as it spread its immense wings, their golden hue majestic and beautiful as the sun caressed the feathers. With one final look, it flew off the wall and straight into the blue sky.

Arcaeus watched until the bird vanished from view. He knew the presence of such a creature was a blessing, but he had yet to figure out how a pair of sandals and a strange bag made of silver were important.

He carried the items past his mother's headstone, sent a final prayer to the God of the Underworld for the safety of his mother's soul and headed back to the impatient horse. He stowed his findings into his saddle bag before mounting the agitated stallion that needed no other instruction than a touch of his heel. The steed bolted straight into a canter and headed back for the main town. He had promised his second-in-command that they would meet and spend the day with a drink in their hands.

The sun shone down on the warrior as he made his way towards the town, fate and destiny now set in motion.

9

Arianna felt like she was so screwed. She hoped that she would wake up and find herself back in bed at her apartment, but when she opened her eyes, all she saw was grey stone above her head. She sat up slowly and winced as her back creaked and groaned from the night spent on the hard cot, then turned her body so she was perched on the side of the simple wooden pallet, its mattress made from itchy wool and straw. Her eyes swept around the room, taking in the rough stone, the wet patches in the corner, and the rat that peeked out from a hole in the wall to eyeball her.

"Ew, dirty little bastard! Shoo! Shoo!" she shrieked.

Arianna shivered and raised her feet from the floor as she considered her situation, such as it was.

She couldn't understand the language and they, whoever they were, couldn't understand hers, so communication was about as much use as a fart in a hurricane. The bull-headed guards who had grabbed her, and who were beefcakes, added to her misery. They hadn't said much, but she could feel the bruises that had started to form on her arms from their rough handling. Arianna got the impression she had been arrested for something, but she had absolutely no clue what.

And she was hungry and thirsty! She had a headache from hell, and it didn't help that she was being kept in a room that smelled like it should really house something of the four-legged variety.

Her arse had gone numb about half an hour ago, but she really didn't feel like getting up and pacing the floor. She had forgotten her sandals and the floor wasn't winning any awards for cleanliness. To be honest, the whole room looked like it hadn't seen or been touched with cleaning instruments in its entire existence. Arianna shuddered. The room was chilly, and it was a chill that seeped into her bones, but she was more concerned about what was going to happen to her. With communication a problem, it heightened her dread for what was to come.

She didn't have her purse, either, which would have come in handy. She at least could have thrown her iPhone at them or introduced them to Angry Birds. Arianna snorted to herself, then giggled. Her laugh rebounded throughout the room, the bare stone walls perfect for acoustics. In another place and definitely another time, she could have sung her heart out. She laughed again and shook her head. Arianna was losing the plot—if she hadn't already lost it.

She placed her head in her hands and tried to think back to what could have happened. One minute, she had been walking through the temple, and the next, she had woken up outside with a sore head, dress all over the place, and was being looked at like she had 'freak' tattooed across her forehead. On top of that, no one spoke bloody English. This was either the most screwed up dream she had ever come up with or she had finally lost all her marbles. Surely, they were the only explanations for what was happening.

Voices echoed down the corridor, followed by the loud thud of boots hitting stone. Arianna bolted to her feet and instantly froze on the cold ground as her toes stepped in something squishy. God knew what it was. She cringed, unwilling to look down and identify the object, and turned to face the door. She held her chin up and prepared herself for anything that would be fired her way. She knew a little of self-defence, and she wasn't above playing dirty. They hadn't nicknamed her 'Bruiser' on the schoolgirl's football team for nothing.

The door was thrown wide open, the solid wood slamming against the wall and causing small bits of loose stone to crumble away, the chips and flakes adding to the large pile of debris already littering the floor. In the shadowed doorway, his bulk preventing any light from filtering through, stood one of the 'beefcakes' from earlier. He would have been a good-looking chap, if it weren't for the ugly sneer plastered across his face as he looked at Arianna like she was a piece of meat in a butcher's shop.

Unease slivered up Arianna's spine, and she struggled to hold her ground against the brute as he stepped into the room. He immediately took what little light and air there was left. Unable to help herself, Arianna involuntarily took a step back to create more space between her and the soldier. Fear seeped into her mind, and it started to set up camp.

His voice, when he spoke, was gravelly, harsh, and far too loud in her already pounding skull. His words, although untranslatable, were laced with disgust as he gestured towards the open door and back to her. His large, dirt-covered hand continued to sweep and gesture in an attempt to be understood. The words were quickly spoken, and he kept repeating the same thing over and over, almost as if repeating the words would finally help her to understand.

"I'm sorry, I don't understand what you are saying."

Arianna attempted to keep her voice steady, but honestly, she was scared shitless. She felt alone and vulnerable and so out of her depth. She had no clue what to do or what was going to happen. In an attempt to calm herself, she grasped at the pendant around her neck, her fingers rubbing over the metal disc in an effort to seek comfort from the words engraved there.

The soldier approached, ignoring her words and confusion, dismissing her outstretched arms that she had hoped would halt his progress, and grasped her upper arm in his large fist. He tugged her forward, hard, causing her to trip over the forgotten debris on the floor. If not for his painful grip, she would have fallen, and honestly, she would prefer to be face down on the ground. Maybe then she would wake up.

He laughed, its cruel sound adding to the pain of his tightening grip. His large fingers dug in and pressed down on the bruises that had already started to show, causing her to cry out. The soldier dragged Arianna through the cold stone corridors, not caring that her feet were bare. She could feel the flesh on the soles of her feet start to shred as he dragged her over fallen stone. They passed other cells that held existing and deceased prisoners, the stench of rot and decay even worse here, and their cries of anguish nearly had her doubling over. Arianna felt sick to the core and utterly petrified.

The soldier continued ploughing forward, his pace quickening and grip growing unbearably tight. The corridor felt never ending. Her feet were now cut, and she knew full well they were bleeding. The only knowledge she gleaned to her predicament was when they passed a fellow soldier. She overheard his murmur, which mentioned a word she had read before. Amazing how one simple word could cause her whole body to shake with fear.

Doulos (slave). She had seen that word many times during her excavations and in many texts, and to hear it spoken now, in obvious reference to her, was freaking her the hell out. A sense of panic started to descend onto Arianna, and she started to tug and pull on the guard's grip, to the point he began dragging her towards a stone staircase that led up to blessed sunshine. Arianna dug her bare heels into the loose dirt and stone in the futile hope of stopping the soldier from his task.

"I'm going to die! Oh my God, I'm going to die!" Arianna whispered the mantra of negativity continuously as she fought the soldier's hold. The closer she was dragged to the steps, the more she could hear the sounds of people laughing and talking, the chatter getting louder and louder. And the overwhelming dread... it was getting stronger.

She knew she was going to be executed. She just knew it. And her overactive imagination was already coming up with gruesome scenarios of her impending death; an axe to the neck, a knife to the throat, gun to the head, only she had yet to see any sort of modern weaponry. Panic had already started to swell within her but had now taken over the rational side of Arianna's brain that would instruct her to keep calm and take in all the facts.

Arianna started to fight harder; she pulled and tugged at the soldier but to no avail. She was half-lifted and half-dragged up the stone steps and out into the bright sunshine. The sunlight blinded Arianna for a split second before a wooden platform, along with a waiting crowd, was revealed. The throng of people all stood with eager smiles on their faces as they turned to look at the approaching victim. A chorus of cheers and whistles, followed by laughs, hit her ears as she continued to fight. She scratched the soldier's arm and hand, quickly drawing blood and eliciting what she assumed were curses from his mouth. Her feral behaviour was much like a cat cornered, but still he refused to let go.

Arianna felt tears of fear and frustration run freely down her cheeks as she fought her captor. She just wanted to close her eyes, wake up back at her apartment and have all of this just be a really, really bad nightmare.

As he turned to face Arianna, the soldier was handed a length of rope by another soldier. She could see it was the other 'beefcake' who had grabbed her at the temple. With a few quick tugs, Arianna's hands were tied in front of her. The first soldier, who she was going to name Arsewipe 1, leaned forward and spoke directly to her face, his spittle flying from his lips as he tugged her closer. This time, his words sounded like a buzz within her brain, and then comprehension dawned. "You won't be so feisty on your back, whore!"

His words, along with the gleam in his eye, was as frightening as his breath was disgusting. Arianna did the only thing she could think of; her left knee lifted on reflex and hit the soldier square in the balls. The crowd went instantly silent as the soldier's groan of pain filled the air. A second passed before he dropped to his knees, eyes closed, and he gasped for breath.

Arianna had only a moment to rejoice in this small victory, as well as now being able to understand the lingo, before she was grabbed by her hair. The sharp pain of hair follicles being removed caused instant tears to spring from her eyes. Harsh words were spat into her face before she was released and pushed forward.

Her face was whipped to the side as the second soldier's fist made contact with her cheek. Pain exploded as Arianna dropped to the ground, the force of the strike easily knocking her off her feet. She hit the deck just as the soldier took aim for a second hit, the breath knocked out of her.

Arianna's head rebounded off the wooden deck, and for the second time, in what could only be a few hours, she was rendered unconscious.

The dark once again took over as she was sent back into sweet oblivion.

10

"Cosmos, surely you jest." Arcaeus shook his head, but the *throb, throb* of its pounding caused him to wince in discomfort. He lifted a hand to cup his forehead.

"No, Arcaeus, I do not. You *were* that drunk, and you *definitely* know how to serenade a tavern." Cosmos grinned as he leaned forward to adjust the bit at his stallion's mouth. The horse pawed at the rough dirt, eager to move forward, as Cosmos waited for his commander and friend to mount his own steed.

The night before had been a celebration of sorts. His battalion had been rewarded for their loyalty and a feast had been prepared. And there had been wine—far too much of it if Arcaeus's head was anything to go by. His men, though, had deserved every bit of the celebration, and for once he had taken part and attempted to enjoy himself. It went a long way to explaining the bad head and now rolling stomach.

"Cosmos, I swear to the gods that is the last time I shall drink again. Ever!" Arcaeus grinned back at his second-in-command and swiftly mounted his stallion, Balios. He threw his long cloak out behind him and nodded as he collected the reins in one of his hands. "Let's go, Cosmos. I'm sure the men are going to need a helping hand getting up this morning."

With a gentle squeeze of Arcaeus's thighs, Balios took the rein and moved into a swift trot. His hooves quickly ate up the road as they headed further into the main town. Arcaeus had no doubt his men would be of little use today; the frivolities would have rendered them incapable of washing or functioning, never mind training. And in all honesty, Arcaeus didn't feel up to much, either. Too much wine and not a lot of sleep made for a bad-tempered, irritable commander.

Despite the thunderstorm going on inside Arcaeus's head, it was a wondrous morning, and Arcaeus hadn't felt this relaxed in years. The constant turmoil inside failed to dampen his mood as it so often did, so he made the most of it. He enjoyed the birds singing in the trees, acknowledged the townspeople that politely said good morning and... just enjoyed the day. He had a feeling it was going to be a blessed one, and good things were around the corner. With a smirk, Arcaeus eyed his friend and winked, before he kicked Balios into a gallop, shouting as he went. "Last one to the town wall supervises the soldiers' wakeup call, Cosmos!"

The short race ended in a draw, and both Arcaeus and Cosmos were grinning like fools as they trotted into the small town. The barracks where the men were housed was just past the centre, right behind one of the main temples, which meant Arcaeus and Cosmos had to ride through the usual morning crowd. Arcaeus's headache had not lessened any. If anything, it had only gotten worse. With a shake of his head, he winced again. It felt like his brain had just rattled inside his skull, and it didn't help when some nitwit in the crowd approached, wielding a drum, its steady beat in time with the thud of his headache.

The crowd was situated around the main stage where

most announcements were made, where the trials of criminals were held, and, of course, where any executions or punishments were performed. Unfortunately, it was also the centre for the town's trade. Items ranged from fruits, animals, and pottery to the one thing that had always turned Arcaeus's stomach. Here, you could buy yourself a slave, a human being, and usually at a reasonable price. Arcaeus had always been brought up to hate this act, but it was normal to his people, so his voice was never heard, even though he complained about the act on a regular basis.

As their horses drew close, Arcaeus could see the main, raised platform. His position on the back of Balios gave him an advantage over the other spectators bobbing up and down; his view of the proceedings was unobstructed. From his vantage point, the other spectators and prospective buyers seemed to be enjoying the show, but no hands were raised, so no bids had taken place yet. Arcaeus turned on his mount to talk to Cosmos, wanting a slight distraction from the spectacle in front, when a loud cheer from the crowd caused Balios to stir restlessly, his hooves pawing at the dirt as his backend reared to the side.

"Calm boy." Arcaeus kept his voice firm as he leaned forward and patted the stallion's neck, before lifting his gaze to roam over the crowd, wondering what could have started the uproar. Previous experience had taught him the auctions were usually boring events and didn't last long at all.

As he leaned back in the saddle, Arcaeus looked across to his second-in-command, ready to gesture that they be off. The words stalled in his mouth as he took in Cosmos' face. His captain's mouth hung open, his skin white, almost as if he had seen a ghost.

"Cosmos, what's wrong, my friend?"

A simple nod of his friend's head had Arcaeus turning on

his mount. His eyes scanned over the crowd, landing quickly on the stage, where he watched the scene unfold before him. One of the town's guards held a young woman in a tight grasp as she struggled and fought fiercely against his hold. As he continued to watch, Arcaeus was stunned as the soldier was felled to the ground by a swift knee to his groin. The soldier fell with both hands tucked between his legs.

A small smile played at the corners of Arcaeus's lips. He didn't doubt the male deserved it. The town guards were notorious for being cruel, especially to any females that came into their care. His smile soon vanished as his jaw dropped with surprise. Shock filled him as he looked up from the guard on floor and the full form and face of the woman came into view.

"No!" Arcaeus shouted. His thighs squeezed around the flanks of Balios as he urged the stallion forward, toward the crowd.

Arcaeus was stunned. It couldn't be! She was dead. He remembered every detail of the day she died, and he had seen her body before it was burned, as was tradition. But the woman who now stood on the stage, defiance set in her posture, was Thalia. His love.

Not caring how this event came to be or who got in his way, Arcaeus urged Balios on faster, controlling the stallion with his thighs he steered through the throng of people. His need to get to her was a desperation he had almost forgotten. The crowd parted quickly when they realised they would get trampled by the stallion, its hooves loud on the cobbled road.

As Arcaeus approached the stage, one leg already thrown over the saddle, he knew Cosmos would be close behind. He watched as the second soldier moved forward and grabbed Thalia by the hair, his anger obvious as he turned her to face him. Arcaeus could do nothing but watch as the soldier's fist flew and connected hard with Thalia's cheek. Her head whipped to the side from the force of the impact.

The moment the soldier's fist made contact with Thalia's face, Arcaeus bolted from the back of Balios and onto the stage, sword already drawn. But he was too late to stop the second fist to her beautiful face, and watched, enraged and despaired, as Thalia slumped to the floor, her head connecting with the wood with a sound that sickened him. Arcaeus already had his sword positioned at the throat of the soldier.

"I suggest you help your fallen comrade and back away from the female." Arcaeus's voice was a quiet growl, his intent clear as he lowered the sword, the muscles of his arms bunching and twitching as fought the need to beat the soldier to within an inch of his life.

His eyes stayed glued to the soldier as he moved around the female to collect his comrade, as he gripped him under the arm and helped him from the ground. Arcaeus continued to watch as they limped from the stage. The felled soldier turned to look at Arcaeus, a smirk on his lips as he gazed from Thalia and back to Arcaeus. The gleam in his eye told him they would meet again, no doubt sooner rather than later.

Arcaeus, aware that Cosmos had already taken on the role of removing the crowd of onlookers, sheathed his sword and took a slow, deep breath. He closed his eyes in an attempt to gain the courage to look down. His heart was pounding within his chest. Nerves he didn't know existed made his hands shake as he finally opened his eyes and looked down at the female.

Her face was hidden from his view by her thick mane of hair, the curls covering and caressing her strangely dressed form. Arcaeus bent down next to her.

By the gods, her form was just as he remembered it. How could he forget? She was made to be loved by him. Slim waist, long legs and curves in all the right places. She was perfect. Perfect for him and him alone.

He moved the hair from her face, and as it was revealed, he inhaled sharply. The bruise from the soldier's hit was already visible. Arcaeus looked his fill. Her beauty, despite the dark purple mark, was obvious. Long eyelashes rested against perfect cheeks, and her lips were dark pink in colour, the bottom one fuller than the top, and above them, a small button nose. Arcaeus couldn't help himself; he swept his fingers down her cheek, a feather light touch that caressed the now black and purple stain marring her skin.

"Arcaeus, my lord, we should move her away from here. May I suggest you take her to your villa. We dare not linger, for I fear we will have the town's local soldiers to deal with if we do."

Arcaeus slid his arms beneath the unconscious female and cradled her small form to his chest as he whistled for Balios. He looked at his second-in-command. "As always, Cosmos, you are correct. Please send word to the barracks; give the men today to recover, but they are to be ready tomorrow."

He slid easily onto the stallion's back, Thalia's body held close to his own. Unable to help himself, he placed a small kiss onto her forehead before he grabbed the reins. His voice was calm and laced with authority as he looked at Cosmos. "Be quick, Cosmos. I prefer to have you at my back whilst she is in this condition. I will take the river road to my villa. Catch up as quick as you can."

"Yes, my lord." Cosmos easily fell back into the mode of warrior as he turned his own steed toward the town centre, and without prompting, it moved into a quick canter. Arcaeus didn't need to watch as his friend did his bidding.

Cosmos was the only person he trusted, so he knew, without a doubt, his order would be carried out to the letter.

Arcaeus tucked Thalia's head firmly against his shoulder as he tightened his thighs on Balios. The steed again showed the purity of his breeding and moved his pace into a swift trot as they headed out of town, toward the river.

11

The sun felt warm on Arianna's skin, which, coupled with the breeze, created shivers that danced up and down her spine. She tilted her head towards the bright rays, taking in its heat and light. There was something about the sun and its warmth that always made her smile. The hotter the better.

Arianna opened her eyes and looked out over the view. She watched as birds and insects swooped and dived around her as she stood in a simple meadow, the sounds of water flowing creating a background symphony. As beautiful and calm as this was, she felt like something wasn't right; a gut feeling that she couldn't quite put her finger on.

So engrossed in the vista before her, she was surprised when a deep voice interrupted her inner thoughts. "Thalia, come back and lie with me. I'm starting to think you prefer nature's company to that of my own."

Arcaeus? Could it be him? Arianna would recognise that voice anywhere. She felt herself frown at the mention of the name 'Thalia'. Who the hell was Thalia?

Arianna turned towards the voice. Unable to prevent

herself, she walked toward the bronzed stud who laid stretched out on a blanket within the meadow. His arms folded behind his head, he regarded her with a sexy smirk that turned up the corner of his mouth. It took Arianna a second to realise that he was, in fact, not looking at her, but through her. She turned her head just as a form, identical to her own, passed through her, causing her whole body to break out in goosebumps. His gaze openly perused the body of the other female, and once finished, sparkled with heat.

Arianna felt her mouth open. "What the hell?" She looked from the stud to the female, eyes wide.

"Of course I prefer your company, Arcaeus. I was merely enjoying my god's blessing, and I relish the feel of the sun on my face."

Arianna focused harder on the scene that played out in front of her. Eventually, she recognised her dream warrior, Arcaeus. She watched as his gaze became more intense. His eyes raked over every inch of 'Thalia', an appreciative smile playing over his lips. He lifted a hand and beckoned her over. "Come, Thalia. Come lie next to me."

Arianna, feeling stunned, watched the female close the distance. Watching this female was like looking in a mirror. The only noticeable difference was the tan of her skin and length of her hair. With an unusual grace, she sank down onto the blanket, folded her legs under her, and smoothed down the chiffon dress. She watched, fascinated, as Thalia's hand swept across his tanned ankle and slowly up the strong muscle of his calf. Arianna refused to miss a moment of this exchange, not sure how to handle the fact she felt a strange, almost jealous sensation. A pricking sense of displacement filled her, and she quickly realised this reminded her of the vision she'd had before the disastrous date.

Arcaeus looked back at Thalia, his eyes full of hunger as he watched each movement of her hand, his breath harsh in the near quiet. "What you do to me, Thalia... Your touch alone sets my blood aflame."

Arianna could only observe as the interaction and intensity between the two increased. She felt awkward, an intruder on something so intimate, and yet she didn't think she could turn away even if she wanted to. The exchange and obvious building heat had her transfixed. As Thalia's hand travelled up and across Arcaeus's solid thigh, a soft voice drifted through Arianna's mind, its lyrical sound a surprise and its presence able to rip her concentration away from the sight of her warrior. She concentrated hard, desperate to hear what the voice was saying, then flicked her gaze back to Arcaeus. His face, as well as the surroundings, became a blur of colour.

Arianna felt herself being lifted, leaving the scene below. She watched as the meadow faded out until nothing remained but an expanse of white. Arianna drifted along, as though she belonged to an unknown current, as the voice continued to fill her mind. It slowly became louder and more defined, its timber deep and smooth, like dark chocolate. The floating became more of a rocking as sense and feeling slowly returned to Arianna's body.

Arcaeus looked down at the unconscious form in his arms for what had to have been the hundredth time. He was still in shock that she was here, in the flesh. Every now and again, he would gently press his lips to her forehead and send a thankful prayer to the gods. His voice was thick with emotion as he steered Balios along the road next to the river, the sun shining bright, its rays reflecting off the turbulent waters as they flowed past. All seemed perfect. Arcaeus couldn't remember the last time he had felt this at peace with himself. This small, beautiful female had instantly put his soul at ease.

Arcaeus eased Balios to a gentle walk and pushed him to the side of the road, knowing it wouldn't take long for Cosmos to catch them up. He adjusted Thalia in his arms and brought her closer. Nothing had felt so perfect. She fitted against his own hard body as if the gods themselves had moulded her specifically for him and him alone. He took a deep breath in and looked out over the river and meadows as once again he sent a silent prayer to his mother in Elyssia, thanking her for teaching him to never give up.

He tugged on the reins and pulled Balios to a stop. He had felt Thalia start to stir, her body going rigid as consciousness quickly returned. He couldn't wait. He was desperate to see her eyes, to see her smiling up at him as she finally recognised him, then realised they were together again.

The gentle rocking had stopped, but Arianna still felt cocooned against a hard, warm body. She felt relaxed and, for some reason, safe as she unconsciously nuzzled the chest her cheek rested against, then froze as her brain caught up with what had happened. Flashbacks of the guards on the stage filtered through her mind, as well as the backhand that had sent her to the deck.

Panic and fear started to take over, and she did the first thing that came to mind; she punched out with her right hand and heard a loud male curse as the arms holding her tightly relaxed a touch. Keeping the momentum, she hit out for a second time and heard, as well as felt, the crunch of cartilage as she hit home. His shout boosted Arianna into action. She wriggled her bottom and felt herself slip from his grasp. She had a second to feel victorious before her feet met with fresh air.

"Ahh, shit!" The curse left her mouth as she tumbled from where she had been held, her body falling through the air and hitting the solid ground, hard. Arianna cried out as her hands and knees connected with the sharp stones that were scattered across the floor. She could feel blood as it started to ooze from the cuts. She turned and started to back up, her gaze shifting toward what she now recognised as a horse. A huge horse.

Her gaze travelled up and up, taking in the sight of the stunningly beautiful black stallion, and finally came to rest on the legs of its rider. Large feet encased in leather sandals lead up to calves that were also covered in leather shin pads. These led to large, muscled thighs that flexed as they gripped the stallion's flanks. Arianna was mesmerised by the flex and play of muscles. She dragged her gaze away from the dark, tanned skin as she continued her perusal upward, her eyes widening as she took in the leather breastplate that covered a huge expanse of chest and what had to be the widest set of shoulders she had ever seen. Arianna's heart was going a mile a minute as she finally looked up at the rider's face and felt her mouth hang open. She was stunned, because there, right in front of her, living and breathing, was the very reason she hadn't been able to sleep or concentrate for months.

"You!" Arianna choked out as she continued to crawl backwards. "You can't be real."

Arianna felt the panic as it started to well up inside of her. A whispered cry escaped her lips as she reprimanded herself, totally forgetting her surroundings and the warrior who was now dismounting the stallion. His movements were stealth-like; his eyes watched her, as if he knew she was on the verge of bolting. She watched as he moved from the stallion's side, his hands held out in a non-threatening gesture.

Arianna's heart pounded within her chest, her breaths coming in gasps as she willed herself to calm and think. She was positive she had finally lost the plot, that or she had eaten something that had sent her into a stupor.

"This is all just a really bad dream. I'm going to wake up back in my room and all this will be just a memory." Her voice was hoarse as she repeated the mantra over and over, even as her eyes locked with the warrior's. They were just as gorgeous as she recalled; a deep brown that somehow melted her insides. She felt tears start to form and shook her head, her hands held out to stop the warrior's advance.

"No! Don't come any closer. You are not real. You are not Arcaeus, because he is a dream. This is a dream! And I'm going to wake up any moment now." Her voice broke slightly as she stumbled back again. Her feet entangled with the light material of her dress, and she once again fell to the ground.

"Thalia, please, my love… this is not a dream. You have been returned to me, by the will of the gods."

Arcaeus's deep voice washed over Arianna and stirred something deep inside. She couldn't stop herself as she glanced up into the dark eyes of the warrior, recognition and emotion obvious in the orbs as he started to slowly move forward.

"Thalia, let me help you." His voice cut off as the sound of pounding hooves approached, the moment of peace ruined. Arianna grabbed hold of her skirts and stood, wincing as blood still oozed from the cuts to her knees and hands, her mind full of fear as she remembered the guards from the prison. Their promises of hurt and abuse still fresh in her memories.

Arianna watched as the unknown rider approached at speed, his sword drawn as he pulled his stallion to an abrupt halt and vaulted from the horse. She couldn't take this anymore. With a choked cry, she turned and bolted from the two men.

She had no idea which direction she was headed. All she knew was that she needed to get away. Fear had taken a firm hold and was driving her to move. Skirts in hand, she just kept running, fully aware that she was being pursued.

"Thalia! Stop!" Arcaeus's voice thundered as he tried to stop his female from running away. They were so close to the riverbank now, and the recent rains had made the area treacherous. All he could do was run after her and hope she came to her senses.

He had been so close to calming her down and getting her back into his arms, and then Cosmos had arrived, still fresh from his skirmish with the guards, and she had taken one look and bolted. He would have to remember to have a word with Cosmos about what had happened, but that would have to wait.

His sandaled feet hit the ground hard with each step as he chased down his female. Cosmos wasn't far behind, but he remained on horseback, bringing Balios with him.

Arcaeus winced again as he felt blood drip from his nose. The punch to the face had surprised him. There hadn't been a warrior yet who had caught him off guard, yet this fragile, beautiful creature had, and even though he would sport a black eye, he was proud in knowing his woman was a fighter.

Returning his thoughts to the here and now, he called out. "Thalia, for the love of Aphrodite, stop!"

His voice echoed around the meadow as he saw her slow and turn, obvious tears running down her cheeks. They made his heart twist. All he wanted was to take her in his arms, protect and comfort her. The fear in her eyes was almost too much to bear.

---

*A*rianna stopped not far from the edge of the riverbank after she peered over the edge of the hundred-foot drop into the raging waters. She couldn't catch her breath as she turned and faced her pursuers.

"My name is not Thalia," she said quietly as Arcaeus approached with obvious caution, his head tilted as he waited for her to continue. "My name is Arianna, and I—ah, shit!"

Her voice quickly turned to a scream as the bank below gave way; the crumbling mud and grass fell into the raging waters below. Arianna reached out and grabbed hold of some of the remaining damp earth, her fingers digging into the mud in a desperate bid to hold on. "Help! *Please* help!"

Arianna heard the shouts of the warriors as they raced closer and used all her strength in her efforts to pull herself up the bank. Tears streamed down her face, and Arianna looked up as Arcaeus approached, his hand held out as he edged carefully toward her, his own fear evident.

"Here, take my hand. All will be well."

Reaching up, Arianna cried out as their fingertips brushed briefly. The contact sent sparks up Arianna's arm, just as the remainder of the bank gave way, plummeting Arianna into the freezing waters below.

---

*A*rcaeus could only stand and watch as her head disappeared beneath the icy depths, the current grabbing hold.

The only thing that prevented Arcaeus from falling into the river as the remainder of the bank gave way, were the strong arms of Cosmos holding him up and dragging him to more stable ground. Arcaeus couldn't tear his eyes away from where his woman had been. One minute she was there, the next she was gone.

Their touch had been so brief, yet earth-shattering.

He closed his eyes as the memory of her face appeared. He thought of her silent scream as she had fallen, and it ripped a cry from his own throat.

"No!" he shouted as grief again swamped him. "No!" He tried to fight the hold on him but couldn't shake Cosmos' grip. His hold was too strong, the bear hug holding true as they sat in the damp grass.

"Arcaeus, my friend, calm yourself. We need to hurry. We can follow the river to the shallows, further upstream, and we will find her." Cosmos' words, laced with determination, were slow to sink in. Arcaeus felt the breath leave him as he finally realised what his friend was saying—that there was still hope.

He calmly shook off the hold Cosmos had on him and stood. With a look of determination, Arcaeus strode over to Balios, and in one swift movement, he was saddled.

"I pray you are right, Cosmos, because if I don't find her, Hades himself will be hearing from me."

Cosmos watched for only a second as his long-time friend and commander urged his stallion into a gallop, following the river's course. Nothing would ever make him forget the fear in the woman's eyes as she held out a hand for Arcaeus to help her, or the grief in his commander's eyes as he watched her fall. If the woman didn't make it, then it would take the gods themselves to keep Arcaeus in this life. He had known about Thalia, had seen the aftermath of Arcaeus losing her when she had been sacrificed. It had taken his friend a long time to deal with the loss.

With a nod to himself, determined to help his friend with all he had, and a prayer to the goddess Aphrodite, Cosmos returned to his own steed. Mounting just as swiftly as his commander, he urged it to follow Arcaeus and Balios.

12

"Thalia, you have been summoned," Aigle called from inside the temple. "Immediately, Thalia. He is waiting on you."

The priestess hurried past with arms full of flowers as Arianna stood staring blankly. Great, another vision or memory or whatever they could be called. In all honesty, Arianna had had enough of these random windows into another life, where she had no control. She had also had enough of being un-bloody-conscious all the damn time.

She moved toward the inner temple and followed the graceful form of Thalia. A part of Arianna was hooked—she wanted to see and learn more—but her other part really wanted to be back home. She wanted to be back lounging on the sofa, watching stupid movies and daydreaming.

As she entered the temple, she was overwhelmed by the use of gold. It shone everywhere and decorated nearly every item.

A small old man hurried toward Thalia; worry etched on his face. "Thalia, come. Do not tarry, child. Apollo himself has seen fit to visit us."

She watched as Thalia nodded in response and, with speed, followed the priest past brightly decorated columns and wall reliefs until finally reaching a brightly lit room, where, upon a golden throne, sat a man.

He was gorgeous, all bronzed skin and muscles, very much like Arcaeus. But he oozed power. It pulsed around him.

Arianna moved to the side and watched as Thalia slowly lowered to her knees. Once rested on the floor, she bent her head in deep respect. Arianna felt helpless as she watched the scene before her unfold.

"Thalia, my priestess, welcome. You may stand, my dear."

As she stood, she kept her head bowed, her lilting voice answering, "Thank you, my lord. You bless me so with your presence. What does my lord require of me?"

She waited patiently for his reply, but Arianna couldn't help herself as she stepped from side to side. Patience was never one of her virtues.

"Ahh, Thalia, you are a very promising priestess, and you have served me, thus far, perfectly, but I require a gift, if you please." Finally, Thalia looked up, meeting the gaze of the god. Arianna felt an instant dislike for the deity. All the muscles and good looks were worth nothing when his eyes were filled with malice and hate.

She saw Thalia nod in response, her posture clearly betraying her nerves. "Of course, my lord. How may I serve you better?"

Apollo's smile widened, and his power seemed to amplify throughout the room, almost a visible energy. Arianna and Thalia's bodies both shuddered in sync, and she knew then that it wasn't just her who was scared.

"Excellent." With a flick of his fingers, black ribbons appeared, tied around Thalia's wrists. Her gasp filled the room as she looked from the ribbons to the god in front of her, and her eyes glistened with unshed tears.

"Thalia, you pledged your life to serve as my priestess, and as such, in seven days' time, when the sun is at its highest, your life thread will be cut. This is my command."

Arianna covered her mouth with her hand as Thalia did the same. Tears fell steadily from their eyes as the god smiled and vanished in a flash of light. Sobs filled the room, their echoes rebounding from wall to wall.

Arianna felt herself lose focus of Thalia as, once again, the vision faded, leaving behind bright, white light everywhere. Arianna wasn't sure she wanted to wake up, not after her experiences so far.

Arcaeus felt fear. Not just the fear that came with going into a battle, but a deep down, heart-wrenching fear that, if he were a lesser man, would have frozen him in his tracks. He knew he was pushing Balios hard as they raced alongside the river. His eyes glued to the swirling waters, he hoped and prayed he could catch sight of Thalia.

He pushed Balios harder as they approached the bend in the river, a small area that eddied out to create calm, bathing waters. The stallion hadn't even stopped before Arcaeus vaulted from his saddle. His feet hit the ground at a run, and he headed straight into the water.

He hoped he had ridden fast enough to get ahead of Thalia. He dove under the water, feeling and searching. He gasped as he resurfaced, then took in another huge breath before he went under again. He battled against the current, all his strength channelled into pushing his body to its limits.

Arcaeus once again surfaced, his frantic search finally

snagging on a flash of lilac. With haste, he dived and made his way under the water to a small group of rocks. They protected the waters behind from the torrent of waves and, by the will of the gods, also protected Thalia's weak form. Arcaeus loosed a breath as he approached her, her body floating face down. As gentle and as quick as possible, Arcaeus took her small form in his arms and waded back to shore.

Her lips were blue, and her face pale. Arcaeus swept her long locks away from her face before bending down, listening for any heartbeat. He took both hands and started to push down on Thalia's chest, hoping he could expel any fluid from her lungs. He was desperate. He had to save her.

"Come on, Thalia, breathe for me... Please, my love, I can't lose you again." Arcaeus pushed down harder, willing Thalia to show any signs of life. A thunder of hooves signalled Cosmos' arrival.

"Arcaeus, my lord, is she..." He left the question to hang in the air, watching his commander fight for the female's life.

A twitch of limbs told Arcaeus of Thalia's life force returning, followed by extreme coughing as she emptied her lungs of the river water. He hooked an arm around her shoulders and brought her close to his chest. He felt his arms start to shake as adrenaline from her rescue started to wear off.

"Thank the gods." He brushed more hair from her face and kissed her head as he made eye contact with Cosmos, seeing his friend's shoulders sag in relief. He looked down once again at Thalia's face, smiling as she snuggled into his chest. It made his heart swell.

"Mm, five more minutes, please, Sonia. It's my day off." Arcaeus looked at Cosmos. A frown marred both of their faces at the strange words Thalia spoke before she drifted back off into unconsciousness. Arcaeus nodded to Cosmos, an indication to fetch his horse, as he lifted his female into his arms. Even though she was sopping wet, and bruises were dotted across her face—as well as numerous cuts coating her hands and her knees where she had scraped them back at the town,—she was still stunning.

He kept her close as he mounted Balios. A swift whistle had the horse easing into a steady walk. "We go straight to my villa, Cosmos. I want her home and safe."

Cosmos grinned as he watched Arcaeus with the female. "Naturally, my friend. I will, of course, come with you." Cosmos had a feeling that this female would not be the Thalia Arcaeus remembered, not if the black eye and swollen nose he sported was anything to go by. This female was different, and something he knew for a fact his friend needed.

13

Birdsong was the first sound that penetrated Arianna's ears as her mind finally came back from the abyss. This was followed by the feel of gentle swaying. But what she found most strange was the feeling of warmth. She was being held by someone; carefully, but tight enough that she couldn't move.

She kept her eyes shut as she became more and more conscious, not wanting to alert her… well, she wasn't sure what she should call him. Rescuer? Kidnapper? The last thing Arianna could remember before the sharp pain of the cold water was him, her warrior, but she must have had one of those funny dreams again.

She found it continually hard not to move, so she tried to listen to what was happening around her. The swaying, she soon realised as she listened to the sound of hooves connecting with the ground, was due to being on a horse.

Unable to help herself, she took a somewhat silent deep breath in, and froze as she instantly recognized the smell. It triggered memories she couldn't quite place. As though she had dreamed them but couldn't remember the details. Whatever the smell was, it was pleasant and soothing.

Arianna took another deep breath in. She could feel and hear the loud thud of a heartbeat beneath her cheek as it rested against the stranger's chest. The slow, steady beat was soothing and strangely put her at ease. For some unknown reason, Arianna felt no fear. It was as if something inside her recognised this person and knew, without a doubt, that they wouldn't hurt her.

She was so focused on the beat in this stranger's chest that Arianna didn't notice the horse had stopped moving, not until the stranger held on to Arianna a little bit tighter. A male voice broke the silence and forced her heart to leap into her throat. It almost caused her to call out in surprise. But Arianna wanted the stranger to think she was still unconscious, and it was getting more and more difficult with each passing minute.

"That's far enough, Balios. Just calm yourself."

Balios? Who was Balios?

Now she recognised the stranger that held her so tenderly, why wasn't she panicking or fighting to get away? Arianna should be screaming and squirming, desperate to get out of the embrace, but she wasn't. She was simply comfortable and very content. She just felt safe.

At last there was movement. Arianna was cradled like a child as he dismounted. She attempted not to sigh when he kissed her on the forehead. Honestly... she thought it was sweet. She had never had a guy be sweet to her, so she was simply going to enjoy the moment.

His footsteps crunched on the gravel underfoot as he carried Arianna's supposedly unconscious form. Her mind went over how impressive his strength was. No man had ever carried her without hurting themselves. Her next silent breath held with it the scent of him, the smell so comforting and male. She felt a touch drunk on it and had to really concentrate on not giving away her state. She just didn't feel brave enough to face him yet, this strong, tasty-smelling stranger.

His footsteps stopped. Arianna was unable to sneak a peek at their location as he had moved her, so her face was now in full contact with his slightly hairy chest. Dear God, Arianna couldn't help but wonder if he tasted as good as he smelled.

The silence was off-putting but soon forgotten as Arianna's mind strayed back to the events of the past hour or so. One minute, she was in the temple of Aphrodite, then she got herself arrested, and then she was drowning. Finally, she found herself in the arms of a man who had carried her on a horse and was now just standing still while he held her, as if waiting. Arianna felt her nerves start to fray as she just lay there. She felt herself getting more irritable as each second passed.

It was starting to become unbearable when he finally started moving again. She could feel the slight bulge of his biceps as he adjusted her position, then she felt her stomach lurch as he dropped her. Her body hit the water and she went under. Again!

Caught off guard, her mouth and nose filled with water, and her arms and legs flailed as she tried to right herself and reach the surface. Arianna felt her dress tighten around her body as she twisted and turned, its weight dragging her down and keeping her under the water. Soon, but not quite soon enough, an arm snaked around her waist and pulled her up to the surface, until she was against a ridiculously hard and muscular body.

Gasping for breath, Arianna let rip. "What the fucking hell? Why did you do that?" she yelled at the man's chest before tipping her chin up, and up, to meet his gaze.

Sweet Jesus, it was him. The rest of the harsh words Arianna was about to deliver got caught in the back of her throat. She had to be dreaming still, or maybe she'd hit her head harder than she thought. There was no way she was standing in a bathing pool, dripping wet, and facing the sexiest man she had ever seen. And who also happened to be currently haunting her dreams.

God, he was perfect. This dream had to be the most realistic one so far, and this was a dream… wasn't it?

"You," Arianna breathed as her gaze locked with his. The deep brown of his eyes had her mesmerised as she placed her hand on his chest and instantly felt his warmth and strength. This couldn't be real.

"I have got to be dreaming again," Arianna whispered as she continued to look into his eyes, her heartrate going at a rate of knots.

14

May the gods be blessed, she was stunning. Arcaeus's gaze raked across the alluringly wet form of his woman, her hair plastered to her shoulders and face. He actually felt jealous of it. He wanted—no, he desperately needed to be that close to her. And that dress… He licked his suddenly dry lips.

Arcaeus had known she was awake and only thought to play with her a little. He just didn't understand why she had pretended not to be. What a mistake that master plan turned out to be.

The material of the dress clung to every inch of her body, making Arcaeus instantly rock hard, especially when he noticed her breasts. His eyes zeroed in on her nipples, standing to attention due to the cold water, the hard nubs peeking through the material as if begging for his attention. And by the gods will, attention they would get if she didn't say something or move. Unable to stop himself, Arcaeus lifted his hand and gently traced a finger down her cheek, returning her gaze, hypnotized by the green of her eyes and the lips he was so eager to taste.

"Thalia." Arcaeus's voice was just a whisper. "May the gods be blessed, Thalia. I have waited long enough for you to return to me."

With those words, Arcaeus lowered his head and pressed his lips to hers. He moved them slowly, then slid his tongue over the seam, its actions begging for entrance.

Who the hell was Thalia? That was the first question that raced through Arianna's mind as she watched him lower his head. The second was: he was going to kiss her? Finally, another kiss from the god that had haunted her dreams, both day and night, another kiss that could make this dream possibly match her fantasies.

The minute his lips touched hers, she felt herself falling into an abyss that only he could rescue her from. Almost instantly, she was drunk on his taste, and Arianna was unable to resist opening up to this god as his tongue slid across her lips and sought—no, demanded—entrance. Arianna lifted her other hand to join the first and clutched at his chest. Her mind took a leap into the backseat as she leaned into the kiss, and her fingernails dug into the soft leather of his breastplate as lust and passion took over.

A loud moan broke the silence, followed by a more masculine one, and Arianna realised she was the source of the first. Not given time for embarrassment, his large hands gripped her waist, and she was pulled flush to his hard, solid body, nothing separating them. Thigh to thigh, stomach to stomach, and pelvis to pelvis.

Arianna was unable to hold back a gasp as she felt the evidence of his passion. Dear God, that felt huge. Arianna, convinced she was still dreaming, finally decided to release her naughty side and, tightening her grip, she attacked

Arcaeus's tongue with her own. She ground her pelvis against the hard ridge of his erection. This simple act added fuel to an already roaring flame, and Arcaeus's hands travelled down her body to grip her arse as he deepened the kiss further. Arianna was in heaven, and there was no way in hell she wanted to wake up.

"Thalia," he whispered as he moved his lips to kiss her cheek and nibble along the line of her jaw. "For the love of Apollo, woman, you could tempt the gods themselves to stray. I have sorely missed your taste."

Arianna pulled back from the most heated kiss she had ever received. Arcaeus's words and their current location rang alarm bells in Arianna's head. Taking a step back, she stood and faced the cause of her frustration over the past six months. The water, cooling on her skin and clothes, caused her to shiver, and Arianna wrapped her arms around her waist as her feet walked her backwards. She was forced to sit on the cold stone as her legs hit the edge of the pool.

"Stop right there, Arcaeus. My name isn't Thalia. I'm dreaming again, right?" She watched his brow furrow, and her gut tightened as she waited for him to reply.

"Thalia, that is your name, and no, dreaming you are not. Although, to have you back in my arms is almost dreamlike." His words, whilst they sought to offer comfort, still managed to cause alarm.

Arianna shook her head, her response slightly fearful. "My name is not Thalia. It is Arianna. And I must be dreaming. You are not real!"

She held out a shaky hand and pointed a finger at Arcaeus. "You only appear in my dreams! You are a figment of my imagination." Her voice started to squeak, and panic began to set in. She tightened her arms around her body as the damp clothes caused another shiver to tumble down her spine.

Confusion slid across his features as he tried to process Arianna's ramblings. "But you are my Thalia. You have been returned to me." He stepped forward, his hand outstretched, as if he yearned to touch her skin again. "The gods saw fit to return you to me, my woman. My skills and victory in battle have been rewarded."

She held up her hand to stop him as she stood and jabbed a finger into his broad chest. She took several deep, calming breaths. "Just stop right there, buddy. I can't think straight when you crowd me."

Her eyes lifted to meet his and widened as the deep brown orbs flared with desire. Her breath caught in her throat as she watched the direction they took. The silken fabric was plastered to her body and showcased all her assets, especially her breasts and perky, cold nipples. Gasping, Arianna brought her arms up to cover herself. At the same time, she fired a glare in Arcaeus's direction.

"Wait just a damn minute. Let's get something straight." Arianna felt her nerves fray even more as Arcaeus's eyes remained cast down, toward her breasts. "Oi! My eyes are up here."

She waited until they finally met her own. The sheer lust alone caused her heart to stutter and then kick into a full-out gallop. She had never in her life had a man look at her like Arcaeus was doing now.

Taking yet another breath, she tried to refocus her thoughts and speak without squeaking.

"My name is not Thalia. It's Arianna. And as I've said before, you cannot be real because I've only ever seen you in my dreams." Unable to hold his gaze anymore, Arianna took a slow sweep of her surroundings. The pool she was sat beside was in the centre of a small courtyard. The sun beat down on the bricks of the surrounding buildings, and it made them burst with life, their red hues sparkling under the light. The main building stood to the right. It was a single-storey structure, simple in design, with a large doorway, open and inviting. Even though the interior looked dark, she could just recognise the outline of a low bed surrounded with muslin to stop any insects from attacking the occupant. Other doorways gave access to different parts of the main building, giving the impression of status and wealth. A small archway to the left of the courtyard led to what she could see was a small garden. The brief glimpse showed her beautiful flowers in full bloom. Her current location, as she suspected, was the private bathing pool that went with the bedroom she had seen.

Arianna turned her gaze back to Arcaeus and felt herself start to panic, but there was nothing she could do about it.

As if he sensed her distress, Arcaeus moved forward again and ignored the outstretched hand meant to halt him. Their eyes met once more before Arianna asked, in a whispered voice, already dreading the answer, "Where am I?"

Arcaeus turned and faced his friend, who had kept back, giving him space with his woman before he answered Arianna's question. He felt no remorse in kissing his woman in front of him. They had been allies too long to let something as trivial as passion embarrass them.

"Apologies, Cosmos. Please make yourself at home. I will meet with you later."

Cosmos just smiled as he grabbed both reins for the horses. "Very well, Arcaeus. Until later."

He watched as his friend started to whistle while he walked the stallions to the stable.

Arcaeus turned back to the reason for those bruises and answered her honestly. "Athens. You are in Athens." He smiled and tried to erase the worry that appeared on her face. "This is my home, and now yours too. You will have everything you desire."

*A*rianna nodded in response and watched the servants coming and going, as if two fully clothed people, standing in the bathing pool, occurred every day.

Arcaeus held out his hand to Arianna.

"Come, let us get you dried and fed. My servants will see to your every need."

Arianna shook her head and tried to swallow down the panic she felt rising. "Arcaeus, what is the year?"

He frowned and watched her closely as he replied, "Thalia —" Arianna's glare caused him to stutter slightly. "I'm sorry. I mean, Arianna. Arianna, it is the reign of Cimon, who in his wisdom brought Greece together to defeat the Persians." The pride he felt in this declaration showed as he squared his shoulders and stood tall.

"I was blessed to have been chosen to go into battle. In our victory, I was gifted with this villa and the servants. My hope was that one day, I would find my woman, and I would be able to provide protection and a home. For the longest time, she was lost to me. But you have returned." His eyes briefly displayed grief and sadness before he locked the emotions away.

"What happened, Arcaeus? What happened to Thalia?" That name, for some strange reason, stuck in her throat, but she forced herself to approach him.

Arcaeus lifted his hand to cup her cheek, the softness in his eyes showing he needed to touch her, to know she was real. Arianna gave in and realised she needed his touch just as much. It had been so long since a man had been close to her like this.

"You were sacrificed five years ago." Arcaeus's eyes turned cold. "Sacrificed on our wedding day. To Apollo." A myriad of feelings and emotions flowed over Arianna, along with a strange sense of déjà vu. Her instincts yelled at her that something wasn't right as her brain tried to come to terms with the fact that she wasn't home anymore. Home being 2013.

Time travel.

Ancient Greece.

Nice one, Anya. Great mess you've gotten yourself into this time. The reprimand travelled through her skull.

"Oh, shit!" Arianna uttered the simple statement just as, for the fourth time in twenty-four hours, she fell into oblivion.

15

She almost caught him off guard, but luckily, Arcaeus's reflexes were quick from his training, so he was able to catch her before she fell back into the water once more. Not that he minded. He loved having her in his arms. The way she had responded to his kiss was magnificent. Gods... he had wanted that kiss to go on forever.

Arcaeus held her against his chest, careful not to jostle her too much. He walked across his private courtyard, its usual beauty nothing compared to the woman in his arms, and crossed the threshold into his bedroom, where he placed her slender form on his bed. He used his large, calloused fingers to caress her cheek, before he withdrew to a chair in the corner and watched her sleep.

Arcaeus already missed the fire of her green eyes; the way she couldn't hide anything because they gave every emotion away.

Gods, he sounded like a lovesick fool. From what Arianna had said, and her reactions, she wasn't his Thalia, and now he thought back on it, she didn't act the same as his priestess. Thalia had never been so passionate, even when they kissed, and she had never been that wanton. He hadn't complained though. He had wanted her to keep rubbing against him as if she needed him more than her next breath.

His shaft had done its own dance of happiness as soon as he had seen her soaking wet, her lips swollen from his kisses, and her nipples beaded and begging for his touch...

Arcaeus got up from the chair and called for one of his servants. "Watch over her. The moment she awakens, I want to know about it."

With one last look, he left the room, eager to change out of his damp clothing. Arcaeus used the heel of his palm to move his arousal into a more comfortable position. He had to think.

If she had truly come back, then the gods would be aware and wondering why. Arcaeus refused to lose her again. He had made the deal with Apollo for a reason. He just hoped he could hide her and keep her safe until he figured out a way to make the gods themselves see she belonged with him.

Going through to the foyer, he collected his saddle bags and walked into his study. Arcaeus wanted to be close in case she awoke. He was desperate to be the one she turned to for comfort and, of course, love.

Arcaeus called for Cosmos. The events of the day needed to be discussed, and if he was honest with himself, he needed a drink.

Whilst he waited for his second-in-command, he opened his saddle bag and retrieved the strange-looking satchel he had found next to Aphrodite's temple. He was routing through the bag when his friend entered the room.

He looked at Cosmos with a slight frown. The feeling he had in his gut told him this bag had something to do with the female currently asleep in his bed. She was a stunning puzzle, and one he couldn't wait to work out.

"What in the gods?" Arcaeus stared, totally baffled, at the

array of different items that spilled from the bag. He had no clue what they were; small tubes and tubs of substances, a small, shiny egg which couldn't possibly come from a chicken, a purse with some sort of paper and silver coins inside, and a mirror. Well, at least he recognised that. After several confused moments, he put everything back and placed it at the end of the desk.

Pinching the bridge of his nose, Arcaeus sat back and grinned at Cosmos. "Interesting, don't you think?"

Cosmos poured them both a drink and grinned back. "You could say that. I take it you think that small bag is connected to your female?"

"I do, my friend, and it confirms her strange tale. Nothing in that bag is like anything I've ever seen, even on our trips abroad." Arcaeus swirled the amber-coloured liquid in his glass, and his thoughts wandered off. Worry quickly settled in. "In all honesty, Cosmos, I fear that Apollo will try to take her from me, and although she doesn't know me yet, I plan on changing that."

Cosmos tilted his head and asked the question that had been bothering him ever since they had found the female. It concerned him that she had been arrested and was being beaten. "Are you sure it's her, Arcaeus? You say she looks exactly like her but how can you be sure? We did, after all, find her about to be sold."

Arcaeus didn't answer straight away. A long sigh left him before he did. "I know it's her, Cosmos, I feel it here." He slapped a large palm over his chest, right over his heart. "It does not matter in what way she returned to me, just that she did." Arcaeus placed his glass down on the table. He was filled with a determination like never before.

"She will remember me."

Cosmos chuckled and placed his glass on the desk, next to Arianna's bag. "Arcaeus, if anyone is up for the challenge of getting this female to back down, I think it's definitely you. I, however, am going to stay a bachelor. I'm happy as I am."

Arcaeus bellowed out a laugh. "Ha! Cosmos, I look forward to the day you eat those words."

*

*A*pollo, God of the Sun, sat on his dais and gazed about the temple built in his honour. The glitter of gold surrounded him on all sides, and as the God of the Sun, he could never have too much gold.

His fingers drummed out an impatient rhythm on the arm of his chair as he looked at the kneeling form of one of his servants. The news he was receiving was by no means happy. In fact, it was downright fucking annoying.

"She is back, my lord Apollo. I know not how, but whilst I watched Arcaeus, as you instructed, he found her." The servant stopped, nervous and unsure of how the god would react.

"It cannot be her. I made sure she couldn't be revived when I sacrificed her." The god pondered on this new information. If true, this was a problem. He had wanted the warrior's grief to be eternal; a fitting payback for the wrongs done to him. How had Arcaeus done it?

"What else do you know?" he demanded of the servant. The fear that emanated from him was, surprisingly, enjoyable.

"She was unconscious. I believe he found her in the town, about to be sold as a slave, which is all I know, my lord. I swear it." The servant's vow came out as a plea. He was most likely begging for his pathetic life.

Apollo waved his hand in dismissal and watched with scorn as the servant scurried out of his beautiful temple.

"Aphrodite… What are you up to, you meddling bitch? Not to worry. I will just have to adapt my revenge, make it a little more… unique." Apollo grinned to himself and pushed up from his dais. He clicked his fingers, and instantly, a petite blonde girl appeared, dressed in a robe of the sheerest fabric that left nothing to the imagination.

"My lord." She curtsied low and stayed there until he told her to rise.

Apollo grabbed a fistful of the female's hair and pulled her face close to his. "Yes, you will do for now."

He pushed the priestess away and barked out his orders. "Prepare my bath, and then you will await me in my chambers."

With a raised eyebrow and a cruel smile, the sun god watched the young girl scurry away to do his bidding. Her fear increased his arousal as he headed for his bathing pool, eager to relieve a small amount of stress.

It was a hard life being a god.

16

Arianna rolled over and grabbed onto the pillow to bury her head into its softness, the feathers and linen making a dreamy combination. She waited for her alarm clock to go off and ruin what had to have been the best night's sleep she'd had in a while. For once, she hadn't dreamed of stunningly gorgeous warriors with intoxicating kisses.

It took a few seconds before Arianna realised something wasn't quite right. She rose onto her elbows and found she didn't recognise the sheets or the pillows. Or the room, for that matter. The coolness of the linens brought to her attention that she was also naked.

"Whoa! What the hell?" Arianna grabbed the sheet and clutched it to her chest as she peered around the room. When she was sure no one was watching, she slid off the bed, wrapped the sheet tight around her body, and headed over to the window. She pulled back the thin, muslin curtains and saw the pool.

A flood of memories assaulted her mind, and it raced as

she remembered last night's events—before she had once again passed out.

"Well done, Anya, another blackout." She shook her head at her own stupidity and pulled back the curtains fully to reveal the bathing pool that signified she hadn't been dreaming.

"Oh my God." Arianna dove behind the muslin curtain and watched in fascination as Arcaeus himself rose from the bathing pool. Naked! Water dripped down his muscular body, and Arianna just stood there, with her mouth open and closing like a goldfish as she remained transfixed. Unable to drag her gaze away, she clamped her hand to her mouth in an effort to stay silent.

When she had decided earlier that he was perfection, it had absolutely nothing on what he looked like now. She tilted her head to the side and admired the way the muscles in his back moved as he poured water over his head. The water in the pool reached to his hips, so she couldn't quite see his arse, but she would have taken bets that it was perfectly shaped, dimpled, and firm enough that a penny would bounce off it.

Arianna bit down on one of her fingers to stop the moan of enjoyment that threatened to escape her lips. But damn if this man wasn't a walking porn show.

Thankful for the hand that covered her mouth, Arianna let go of the muslin and squeaked as he turned around and walked out of the bathing pool. Dear God above, he could give a horse a run for its money. Her jaw went slack as she watched him dry off, transfixed by the way each and every flex of muscle rippled. She became very jealous of the cloth that was wiping moisture from his body.

Arianna clenched her thighs together as her arousal moved through her body, heating her up from within. Her mind went gutter bound as she stared openly from behind the curtain, as a certain part of his body bobbed up and down with each long, confident stride.

She couldn't believe how perfect Arcaeus was. His body was almost godlike; wide shoulders and a huge chest, obviously defined from lifting a sword, which tapered down to a drool worthy set of abs. Arianna fixed her gaze on his chest, determined to not let it drift further south. Just thinking about it had her lady bits clenching.

Her mind was so focused on perving that she didn't even notice he was making his way towards the master bedroom, which meant he was heading straight in her direction.

Arianna spun on her heel and stumbled across to the bed. With the sheet tightly clasped to her body, she made sure the bed was between her and the rapidly approaching warrior. Her heartrate was already sky high as she watched Arcaeus stroll into the room. She couldn't help but stare, and she squeaked when he turned his back and bent down to collect his clothing from a chair. The man was perfect… everywhere.

Arianna's squeak alerted Arcaeus to her presence, and he slowly turned to face her. His leisurely perusal of her sheet-covered body sent heat to her cheeks—and other areas. Arcaeus took his time getting dressed. His gaze held Arianna's as he made his way around the bed to crowd her against the wall. He stopped in front of her before lifting his hand and stroking a calloused finger down her cheek. Passion-filled energy shot between them.

"I'm glad to see you awake, Arianna. I trust you slept well?" he murmured, his voice deep and rough.

Arianna nodded, unable to form any words, her brain reduced to mush.

"I have an outing planned for us, a way for us to get to know each other." He tilted his head toward a doorway. "You will find help dressing in that room there."

He cupped her cheek and stroked his thumb over her bottom lip, his eyes glazed with hunger as they gazed to where his thumb continued its movements.

"I will await you in the courtyard." With those words and another longing glance, he turned and left the room. Arianna watched his back until he was out of sight before she sunk to the ground.

"Oh my!"

17

Silence stretched between Arcaeus and Arianna as they sat in the cart. The only sounds were the surrounding wildlife and the fall of the horse's hooves. Arianna felt awkward. Arcaeus hadn't said a thing since he had gently picked her up by the waist and put her into the cart. The minute he placed his hands on her, she had started to combust from the inside out. But now she just felt awkward. There were so many questions that raced through her head, but she didn't dare break the silence first.

The first thing she wanted to know was how the hell she had ended up in Ancient Greece—Ancient Athens, to be precise. Not that the archaeologist in her was complaining. That part of Arianna was currently perched on her shoulder, notebook in hand, taking a shit load of notes. Her inner siren sat on the other shoulder and stripped the Greek warrior beside her bare. Gods, the man was sinfully good-looking. In any other situation she should be scared to death that she was far from home in both distance and in time, yet this man had been in her dreams so much lately the fear just wasn't there. In fact, she felt drawn to him.

Arianna sneaked a glance at Arcaeus and was again struck by how sexy he looked. They didn't make them like this back in Manchester.

Damn, Anya, stop it! Every time she looked at him, her mind and body went straight to the gutter.

She forced her eyes away from him and allowed herself to take in the scenery as they slowly moved along the road. This country was simply breath-taking, with fields full of ready-to-be-harvested corn, and a slow, lazy river meandering its way through the landscape, the water sparkling under the morning sun. Arianna leaned forward as they passed a meadow, its flowers a sea of beautiful colours. So engrossed in the view, Arianna didn't realise the cart had stopped until the huge form of Arcaeus stepped in front of her. His sudden appearance almost caused her to jump out of the carriage.

"Sweet Jesus, you startled me!" Arianna sat back in her seat and placed her hand over her chest.

Smiling wide, Arcaeus reached out his hand, trusting in her to take it. "Apologies, Arianna. It was not my intent."

She placed her slender hand in his and let him help her from the cart. She found herself unable to move far before he slid her arm through his before leading her into the very meadow she had been fascinated with.

The voice inside Arianna's head whispered, *it's okay*, as they walked side by side, then went silent once again. Her mind focused on how his arm felt under her hand, the way his muscles flexed, tempting her to give a gentle squeeze.

Arcaeus seemed to realise she was struggling to keep up, and she was grateful when he slowed his pace to match hers. Although his demeanour appeared completely relaxed, she would bet he kept a close watch on their surroundings.

"So, Arcaeus, what do you do?" Arianna asked, needing to fill the uncomfortable silence. His presence alone already made her feel on edge.

"I am a warrior, Arianna. I mainly train until called upon to go to war. Luckily, at this present time we are at peace, so I am not needed." He said all this with pride, his chest pushed out, all male. He continued to lead the way until they reached a small bench that sat on the edge of the meadow, overlooking the river.

Arianna let go of Arcaeus's arm and stepped forward to stand at the edge of the small cliff, unable to stifle the small sound of pleasure that escaped her mouth as she took in the overall vista. Feelings of pure wonder filled her as she took in the majesty of the beautiful sight before her.

"This place is spectacular, Arcaeus, so peaceful. Do you come here often?" Arianna turned to face the warrior and saw him perched on the bench, looking down at his clasped hands, a frown marring his handsome features and making her own heart ache in response.

"Arcaeus, are you okay?" Arianna asked in earnest as she moved closer. Genuine concern for this man filtered through her.

"Arianna, please sit. I think it's time I told you everything. I know you have many questions, and I hope my story can answer some of them for you." His words were polite yet laced with sadness

Arianna nodded and gave him a tentative smile that she hoped would put him at ease. She walked over and slid onto the bench next to him, her body turned so their thighs brushed.

Arcaeus's nostrils flared at the small contact, before he took Arianna's hand and drew small circles on her palm. Arianna's gaze flicked to his face, and she watched as he took a deep breath. His voice, when he spoke, was laced with heartache.

"Six years ago, I met and fell in love with a priestess of Apollo. Her name was Thalia, and she was more beautiful than the gods could comprehend. She was kind and patient, a loyal follower who took her duties very seriously, and as such, wanted to wait until we were married before we consummated our love."

He looked happy as he spoke of his love. Arianna squeezed his hand in comfort and encouragement. He nodded and smiled before he continued. "No one knew about us as we had always kept it a secret, not wanting others to object. She was allowed to marry but would have to leave her position as priestess first. We had discussed it and were set to petition Apollo on the next full moon to get his blessing on our union."

Arcaeus's wide shoulders seemed to sag as his memories took him somewhere that was obviously painful.

"The day before we were due to petition the god and be married, we met at our usual place: the Gardens of the Muses. Only, she didn't run to meet me as she usually did. She stayed sitting down on our bench, her fingers tugging at something on her wrist. As I approached, she looked up at me. I remember the look of sadness and regret that was so obvious in her green eyes—the exact colour of yours, Arianna." He reached out to stroke her cheek, fingers feather light. They sent tingles across Arianna's face.

"It was only then that I noticed she had black ribbons tied to her wrists. The god Apollo, after years of not needing or wanting a human sacrifice, had chosen my future bride."

Arianna moved closer as the pain in Arcaeus's face concerned her. She covered both his hands with her own and turned them over to stroke Arcaeus's battle-roughened skin in an effort to offer what comfort she could.

"The day we had planned to petition Apollo, she was sacrificed, in honour of the god we had worshiped and prayed to for years." With that confession, Arcaeus's look changed. Gone was the hurt warrior, the sad eyes, and instead a steely resolve filled his eyes, banishing the sadness that had been there. The change in his demeanour was simply frightening to behold.

"After months of grieving, I petitioned Apollo for a gift. I asked to become a soul searcher, a gift the god rarely honoured anyone with. He granted my request, and so my search began."

Arianna frowned as she listened. "Search? For what, Arcaeus? And what do you mean Apollo granted you the gift? Are you saying you met him in the flesh?"

Arcaeus nodded, a small smile on his lips as he released her hands. He stood and paced, his next words a little clipped. "Yes, he exists, and yes, I have met the god. My search was for Thalia, for she is my soul mate. We were made for each other."

He bent down in front of Arianna and took her hands back into his own as he looked deep into her eyes. "My search took me to the dreams of my soul mate, into a forest with a white fountain."

He waited patiently whilst his words slowly filtered into Arianna's brain.

"Whoa, what?" Arianna stood quickly, her movement nearly forcing the warrior onto his arse. With quick reflexes, he stood and regained his balance, her hands still held tight in his own.

"What are you saying, Arcaeus?" she asked, her voice a little high-pitched.

"You remember the dreams, Arianna? I wouldn't have been in them if your soul hadn't called out to mine, just as you can feel my own calling to you now. You may have a different name, and be from the future, but you are my Thalia, returned to me after all this time."

Arianna shook her head in denial and stepped back until

her knees hit the front of the bench. Forced to sit back down, Arcaeus's form seemed to overpower her.

"No! I can't be. I'm not from your world." Her mind was a whirlwind as she tried to process the information. Finally, as if giving in, she admitted that this couldn't happen in Manchester or modern-day Athens, and that she quite possibly had really gone back in time.

"I don't believe in gods or soul mates or magic. It just doesn't happen." Arianna felt her body start to shake. Suddenly cold, like a chill had overtaken her, Arianna stood and tried to pace.

"Arianna, please do not deny this." Arcaeus halted her and placed his hand directly over her heart. Arianna couldn't stop herself from looking up into his chocolate brown eyes.

"You feel it here. You have done since the moment we met by the fountain. Your soul recognises its mate." With these simple words, he claimed Arianna's mouth, his tongue demanding and coaxing a response from her. Like he needed to show her just how much this meant to him.

Arianna wanted to resist, and she raised her hands with the intent to push at his chest. But she found herself unable to do so. He was right; her heart ached when she thought of him. She had just never realised it. Deciding to damn the consequences, Arianna kissed him back and poured all her yearning into this one moment.

She decided that even if this was a dream and she could wake up at any point, she would rather have known this sort of passion than not felt it at all.

18

This woman was driving Arcaeus crazy. At first, he was convinced she was going to reject him, and now, she kissed him back like she would die without his lips on hers. He kept her mouth occupied as he manoeuvred them. He sat back on the bench before gently pulling her onto his lap, his hands roaming over her curves. He didn't think he would ever get tired of this woman.

He knew she wasn't his Thalia. She had more passion than Thalia had ever had. They may share looks and certain habits and, most importantly, a soul, but that was where the similarities ended. Arcaeus remembered Thalia as being a quiet, shy and patient woman. This woman was as far removed from that as she could get. This woman was passionate, beautiful, stubborn and very smart. And if he was honest, he was in love with this version of his soul mate already. Arcaeus felt he could be himself with her. He could show her his passions and not have her be frightened of them.

He pulled her harder into his embrace and forced his mouth away from hers to rest his forehead against her own.

"We had best stop, my *Theia*." He smiled as he stroked her hair, pleased at the effect his kisses had upon her. "You make me burn, and I would rather combust in private." His words caused a deep blush to travel up her cheeks, and a small, embarrassed laugh escaped her as she turned her head into his neck.

Unable to release her, he held her tight and stood in one fluid motion. He carried her through the meadow and to the cart, her head still buried in his neck.

"Arcaeus," Arianna whispered against his skin. "What do you mean when you call me *Theia*?"

Arcaeus pressed his lips to her forehead, his answer just as quiet as hers. "My Theia means my goddess, Arianna. You are the one I worship now." Unable to stop himself, he pressed his lips to her skin. He just couldn't stop touching her.

"Come, I still want to show you my home, and maybe look through the markets. I assume women from the future also like to shop." Arcaeus grinned down at the bright red face of Arianna. He coaxed a beautiful smile in response, accompanied by a nod.

"Good! Shopping it is, then, my lady."

---

*A*pollo watched Arcaeus from his dais. The waters of the seeing pool rippled as he flicked a finger into it.

"Well, well, well, he has found her. I must say, this version of my priestess is more pleasing, and definitely more passionate."

The god sat back on his throne, his fingers tapping out a thoughtful rhythm against the arm as he contemplated his next move. He had known Arcaeus wanted the gift of soul searching so he could find his woman. Now he just had to lure him in and make him suffer. The question was, should he use the girl?

Definitely! That sounded like fun.

Apollo stood. His long, lean legs took him across the room, where he reached out with a tanned arm to grab a goblet of ambrosia.A smile crossed his lips. The thought of revenge on the family that had caused so much hurt brought him nothing but pleasure.

Arcaeus's mother, Desma, had been beautiful, easily distracting the god from his duties, and she had been a wonderful lover. Apollo had been sure he would never tire of her, only it was she who had tired of him. Desma had sought him out one day and requested he give her leave of her position as priestess, so that she could marry.

He had been shocked, of course, and, being a kind and gracious god, he had given his blessing. But inside, he had raged with anger that a mere mortal had dared to take what belonged to him. So he may have sent her husband off to a little war that just may have caused him to suffer a mortal wound. The god chuckled into his goblet, then his mood turned angry as he recalled finding out she had already become pregnant. So, he had waited, had observed as her son grew up into a strong and noble mortal, then watched as that brat had the nerve to fall in love with one of his priestesses.

He hadn't needed a sacrifice, but watching the effect losing her had on the son of the woman who spurned him, had been worth it. But now, Arcaeus had found her again, and Apollo could not have that. He was the sun god. He would have the last word.

He threw the goblet at the wall just as the sound of chains being moved echoed from his chambers. The girl was still chained to his bed. Good. He still wasn't done with her, and he had to prepare himself for the priestess. After she watched him kill Arcaeus, he might just keep her alive for a short while. See how entertaining she could really be.

Apollo left the room, sporting a huge smile, and he felt happy for the first time in years.

19

The ride back to the villa was a little tense. Their shopping adventure had been amazing, but the lust from the start of their trip remained. Arcaeus sat ramrod straight as he eagerly encouraged Balios to move faster. As for Arianna, she was incredibly nervous. She couldn't remember the last time she had been this close to a man who wanted to get down and dirty with her. During her past experiences—okay, that one time—her ex had turned the lights off then fumbled in the dark. A few short grunts and bam! That was it. If it hadn't been for that little box under her bed, she was sure she would never have known what an orgasm was.

Arianna knew the reason for her nerves; Arcaeus was all male and obviously knew what he was doing, whereas she was shy and didn't have a clue, other than what she'd seen in erotic films she'd watched with Sonia. For about the hundredth time, she felt a blush crawl up her neck and onto her cheeks.

Arianna turned to watch the scenery again, her thoughts

once more turning through the events of the past twenty-four hours.

To sum it all up, she had gone from being a plain Jane to being the reincarnation of a priestess, who was technically engaged to a Greek warrior. And to top it all off, they were, apparently, 'soul mates'. Arianna took a deep breath and again looked at the warrior beside her. To be honest, she couldn't go far wrong with this guy. Compared to Andrew, this man was a god.

Arianna spent the whole journey back contemplating her confusion. She didn't know whether she would be going back to her time or whether she'd be stuck here, and if she had to return, what would happen with Arcaeus?

Arianna could easily admit that, from what little she had seen, she loved it here. For some strange reason she certainly felt like she belonged here too. And she couldn't deny she was drawn to the man sat next to her.

Her inner resolve had made up its mind: no matter what happened to her, whether she went home or stayed here, Arianna was going to open her heart and soul to this man who, technically, had been a part of her life for over six months already. She just hoped that if she had to leave, her heart could take it, because when she fell, she knew she would tumble hard and fast. If she was honest with herself, the fall had already started.

The journey in the cart was not quick enough. Arianna felt herself getting tenser the longer the ride took. She was convinced Balios deliberately took his time. Bloody horse!

As they rounded the bend, she spotted the villa and her heart decided to start off on a gallop that went faster than Balios. Arianna clenched her hands as they became clammy, and she started to fidget in her seat. She glanced at Arcaeus from under her lashes, hoping he hadn't noticed. He seemed relaxed, except for the grip he had on the reins. She smiled and felt a little more relaxed as she slid her hand over one of his own and gently squeezed.

"Are you okay?" Arianna asked, simply hoping to break the silence.

"I am, indeed, *Theia*. Very much so." His smiled response made her jaw drop. A man that gorgeous should be illegal. The look in his eyes made her stomach flip. It simply stated, *I want you*.

With ease, Arcaeus directed the cart into the courtyard of the villa. He quickly dismounted and made his way around to Arianna's side of the cart, where he offered his hand, ready to help her exit.

The sudden appearance of a servant brought a frown to his handsome features. He turned to help Arianna down from the cart, leaned in close, and whispered, "I apologise. I must see to business, but I will not be long. I will find you."

He grinned at Arianna before pressing his lips to hers. The kiss was quick, but it was enough, and it showed her exactly how he felt. Arianna touched her swollen lips as she watched him stride off to what must be his office, her eyes drawn to Arcaeus's fabulous backside.

"Anya, stop perving." Arianna shook her head and reprimanded herself before she moved into the villa complex, making her way toward the private area. Once inside, Arianna started to nosey around the room. She wanted to feel a little more at home.

Home... Yes, she could definitely call this home. That simple thought made Arianna smile.

After she entered the private rooms of the villa, Arianna peeked into every nook and cranny, satisfying the scholar within her. She covered her mouth and stifled a yawn before she entered the bedroom. Arianna walked past the dresser and stopped suddenly as she recognised her purse, feeling shocked and happy at the same time. Arianna grabbed it, hurried over to the bed, and emptied out the contents. She wondered if her compact and face wipes were still in there.

"Oh yes, get in there. I totally forgot about you." Arianna laughed out loud and pulled the small, foil-covered egg from her purse.

"You, my little friend, are just what a girl needs when she is feeling emotional." Arianna giggled and placed it to one side before she attacked the rest of the bag. She needed to feel a little more like herself, especially before Arcaeus came back.

Arianna sighed as she leaned back into the cushions. The wipes and other things in her bag had worked wonders. With one hand under her head, she contemplated 'the egg'.

"Well, this may be the last one I ever get, so I may as well enjoy it." She peeled off the foil wrapper before licking the very top. She closed her eyes as she moaned in delight. The taste of the chocolate was absolute heaven to her senses.

"Oh, you are so good."

20

As he approached his chambers, he could have sworn he heard a moan. Arcaeus quickened his pace. He stopped before a set of muslin curtains, slid a hand through the material, and peeked inside. From his position, all he could see was Arianna's back.

She was reclined on his bed, stretched out and relaxed, just as depicted in the reliefs of the goddesses. He was still getting used to the idea that his woman was here in the flesh, and more importantly, reclining on his bed, awaiting him.

She moaned again, and his body reacted instantly. His curiosity got the better of him. He walked into the room and stopped at the end of the bed, his face entranced as she licked the brown, egg-shaped item he had seen in her purse. The look of rapture the tiny object brought to her face was exquisite. He wanted to see that look as he brought her to pleasure. And how was this egg doing it? What could it be?

Eager to know, he climbed onto the bed and reclined in the same position.

"Arianna?" he whispered.

*A*rianna squealed with surprise as she opened her eyes to find herself held captive by chocolate brown ones. The interruption caused her to drop the egg onto the covers.

"Oh my God!" Her hand on her chest, she felt her cheeks start to heat. "You scared the shit out of me, Arcaeus."

"Again, Arianna, I apologise, but you seemed to be enjoying yourself so much. Please tell me what it is you are eating." He picked up the egg gently, took a sniff, and turned it this way and that, his forehead crinkled in a frown.

Arianna took the egg out of his hand before it melted and wrapped the base with the remainder of the foil.

"It's chocolate." Arianna waited for Arcaeus to say something, but he continued to just look at her, a small tilt to his lips as he waited for her to continue.

"It's a sweet confectionary, made from the cocoa plant."

A simple nod from Arcaeus told her he sort of understood. He bade Arianna to continue, so she held out the egg and explained, "It's a treat in my time; very sweet but oh so very tasty."

Arianna gently bit the top and broke through the chocolate. She grabbed a loose piece and offered it to Arcaeus.

"Close your eyes." He smirked at her but did as she requested.

"Now, open wide." Arianna grinned as she placed the small piece onto his tongue. She gasped out loud as he sucked her finger and thumb into his mouth, his eyes now open and hot with lust as she removed the digits. Arianna watched as he chewed on the chocolate, his jaw working slowly.

As she waited for his reaction, Arianna brought the egg back to her own mouth. Her tongue dipped inside to lick out the crème filling. Arcaeus's moan had Arianna transfixed. She watched as he ate the chocolate. All the while, his own eyes were pinpointed on Arianna's. The obvious lust in his gaze instantly boosted the arousal that already thrummed through her body.

"Arianna, this is divine." Arcaeus held out his hand and gestured for Arianna to hand over the egg. She was reluctant as she placed the chocolate treat into his hand. She was prepared to beat him or cause some harm if he had the nerve to eat it all. It was Cadburys!

Arianna tilted her head and watched as Arcaeus broke off small pieces of the egg, then scooped the filling onto his finger. He crooked it at her and patted the space next to him, a clear hint for Arianna to move closer. She scooted across the bed and settled flush against his body, her head now resting on his shoulder. Already she felt her cheeks flush and butterflies starting to take root in her stomach. All of a sudden, Arianna started to feel shy.

Arcaeus turned on the bed and placed an arm above Arianna's head. The corners of his lips curled up into a seductive grin as he spread the filling on his finger over Arianna's throat. He carried on the trail to the upper part of her chest, and with a look that could make any girl turn to mush, lifted his finger to her mouth and rubbed the rest of the decadent fondant across Arianna's lips.

Arianna watched, her breath held, as he bent his head and started to lick across her chest, cleaning up the gooey mess with his tongue. She felt her heart race as he gently assaulted her neck. Unable to stop herself, she groaned. The wonderful sensation he created caused goosebumps to break out all over her body.

"I was wrong, my *Theia*. It tastes even better on you, better than the gods' ambrosia." His voice was low and husky, each syllable laced with desire.

Arcaeus moved his lips slowly along the slender column of her neck, ensuring he licked up every drop of the creamy filling from Arianna's skin. He took his time, with small bites and kisses to her jaw, before he took full control of her mouth. Natural instinct and raw need kicked in, and she reached up to dig her hands into his hair. She held him close and kissed him back, showed him with her mouth how much she wanted him.

This was it; the passion Arianna had always felt was missing from her life. Arcaeus, her wonderful dream warrior come to life, ignited the flames in her body and made her crave more.

Her body on fire, she arched into Arcaeus. She needed the warrior even closer as the kiss became more and more frantic. Years of pent up need forced its way to the forefront and created wanton thoughts and actions.

"Arcaeus, please." Arianna's voice sounded needy as she forced her mouth away from his. Her hands moved to undo the ties on his leather breastplate, eager to see and taste his delectable skin.

Moaning loudly, her disapproval evident, he moved off the bed to stand beside her, where she was sprawled unladylike. He reached down and stroked her cheek as his gaze travelled up and down her body. Slowly, Arcaeus shrugged off his breastplate, revealing his upper torso. Arianna's mouth instantly went dry as she stared at the defined muscles, wide shoulders, broad and powerful pecs that she had the overwhelming urge to lick. His dark nipples peaked, surrounded by a small dusting of light brown hair that continued down the centre of his chest and snaked into a trail that led to the sexiest eight pack Arianna had ever seen. Each ridge of muscle demanded her attention. She couldn't help but rise onto her elbows to get a better look.

Arcaeus leaned forward and released the brooch that held

Arianna's Chiton in place. The material fell and pooled at her waist, and with her breasts now revealed, she had to fight the urge to cover herself as she forced back years of shyness. She felt her nipples bead and harden under the intensity of his gaze, and it made her feel sexy.

Arianna leaned back and ran her foot up and down Arcaeus's calves. Inside, Arianna's body was shaking. On one hand, she was extremely nervous, but on the other, she was desperate for this man, to the point she let her inhibitions vanish.

Arianna sat forward and placed her hands on his hips. Her fingertips caressed the skin above the waistband of the kilt, the material seated low on his hips and highlighting the ridge of muscle that lead downwards and disappeared under the fabric. Arianna placed a small kiss just above his belly button and tried to figure out how to get the troublesome garment undone without looking stupid.

She looked up into those deep brown eyes as she slid her hands down the kilt until she reached the hem. Her hands slid underneath and tentatively caressed their way along the warm flesh of his thighs, the fine hairs brushing against her palms. She loved the feel of his muscles; the way they flexed and contracted as her hand moved higher.

Arianna knew her own feelings of desire were shared by Arcaeus. His eyes were dilated, and his breaths were just as ragged as hers. She kept her eyes locked with his as her fingers brushed against the short, coarse hairs that surrounded his heavy sac, before edging ever so slightly higher.

The catch in his throat told Arianna just how much her touch affected her warrior as she slowly took Arcaeus's semi-erect cock in her hand. The size itself made her a little nervous. Her eyes widened as it hardened further within her grasp.

Arianna bit her lip as her conscience made a small appearance and asked what the hell she was doing with her hand up a man's kilt. The siren perched on her shoulder got her pom poms out and cheered her on.

"Oh, Arcaeus," Arianna breathed as she pressed her lips to his skin and licked his lower abs. The hold his gaze had on her was too much, the emotion just too overwhelming.

"You had better get this kilt off and do it quick." Arianna's breath was ragged as her hands tugged on the clothing in question. Her voice sounded throaty, nothing at all like her, but she was finding it hard to string her words together.

Arianna frowned as Arcaeus stepped away. Her hand reluctantly detached from her new toy, and she started to doubt whether Arcaeus wanted her. She watched as Arcaeus unclipped a small pin at his left hip and, all too slowly, unwound the material from his hips and dropped it to the floor.

"Gods above." Arianna's mouth became dry, and her mind went blank for a second before she focused on the perfection that stood completely naked in front of her. Her eyes zeroed in on his groin, her hungry gaze focused on his cock jutting out, long and thick, from a thatch of dark brown hair.

His thighs alone were perfect; solid and muscular, obviously built from years of training and horse riding.

Arianna's first thought? Where the hell was a tub of Nutella when a girl needed one? Her second was simply, where to start? Arianna stood up from the bed. She needed to get to Arcaeus, who was in the middle of the room. She took a step but tripped as she became tangled in the copious amounts of material from her dress. It wrapped around her waist and feet and caused Arianna to fall to her knees.

Oh, good God! How embarrassing. Arianna sat on the floor, breasts in full view as she tried to battle her way out of the material. She avoided looking up. She didn't want to see

Arcaeus, who was no doubt laughing at her. And she was afraid that all he would see was her not so skinny body parts. Deep inside, she begged for a hole to appear, to swallow her up and save her from the embarrassment.

Arianna gasped as warm hands grasped her own and effectively stopped her from grappling with the material. His large, tanned hands made easy work of the chiffon, and within seconds, Arianna was free. Not to mention, completely naked and at his mercy.

Arcaeus took hold of Arianna's hands and helped her to stand, his movements quick as he pulled her flush against his body. Large arms wrapped around her waist, wrists locked, and her backside was cupped within his palms. The feel of his cock pushing against her belly had her pussy throbbing.

Arcaeus bent his head to her own. She met him halfway and brushed her lips, gently at first, against his, before the kiss deepened and became heated. Their tongues duelled and fought for dominance.

Arianna clutched at his shoulders, her nails breaking the skin and causing small welts as their desire escalated. Her body heat rose to match his as the hairs across his chest, stomach and thighs brushed against her skin and started a tingling feeling so erotic she never wanted it to end. He moved his hands lower and used his strength to lift Arianna up without breaking the kiss.

In two strides, Arcaeus was back at the bed, and he gently lowered her until she was sat on the sheets, before stepping between her parted thighs. Arianna used the opportunity to explore Arcaeus's body. She placed one hand against the flat of his stomach, and the other she wrapped around his fully erect cock; the feel of the solid girth, engorged and sheathed in soft velvet, so enjoyable she wanted to touch and play with it for hours.

Arcaeus's groan was the only encouragement she needed.

Arianna, with a tight grip, slowly moved her hand up and down, his girth so thick her fingertips barely met.

She moaned as Arcaeus slid his hands into her long hair, deft fingers teasing the soft tendrils as he gently rocked his hips against her hand. Arianna felt braver than ever before as she looked into his eyes and released her hold on his shaft. She moved her hands to her breasts and offered a seductive grin as she plumped and squeezed them together. Arcaeus grinned in return as he realised her intent.

He took his large cock in his hand and groaned as he pumped up and down, his lust-filled gaze fixated on her breasts. The sight of this warrior, thick shaft in hand and stroking himself, made Arianna soaked and more than ready for him. She moved to perch on the end of the bed and licked her lips as Arcaeus slid his huge cock between her breasts. She pushed them tighter together and watched as he thrusted slowly. The crown of his cock pushed through her breasts with each up thrust, enough that she could suck and swirl her tongue around the tip.

Arcaeus moved his hips and set a quickened pace. She sucked even harder on the weeping crown, and it wrung deep and guttural moans from her warrior. She couldn't get enough of this man; the taste of him was addictive, and her own moans of pleasure echoed around the room, in tandem with his.

Her mouth was like heaven, and her breasts... Gods, Arcaeus had very nearly released like a youth when she had first touched him. The only thing that saved him from embarrassment was his ability to stay focused and push away the image of her covered in his seed.

Arcaeus was desperate to be buried deep inside her. He

wanted to show Arianna, in the simple ways of man and woman, how much he desired her. But he also knew she was nervous, so, for her, he would make sure he lasted and took things slow. Was she a virgin? Was he her first? If she were, he would make this as pleasurable as possible.

By the gods, he nearly lost all control again. Her breasts surrounding his shaft was the most erotic thing he had ever seen, and he groaned with unashamed pleasure as the tip of his cock shuttled in and out of her mouth. Arcaeus mentally recited the mantra, *I will not explode. I will not explode.* It went round and round in his head and helped him take back some control, but he knew he wouldn't be able to keep it up for long.

Arcaeus wanted this woman, *his* woman, with a passion he had never known before. She set him aflame; the smell and touch of her skin, the feel of her small hands on his body, her kiss… all reduced him to a pile of soft clay.

"Oh, blessed gods, Arianna, your mouth… Gods!" He felt his head drop back as her simple, yet heavenly assault continued. With a will he had no idea he possessed, he took a deep breath and used all his resolve to move away from her decadent mouth. Unbidden, a chuckle escaped him as he caught her pouting expression. It soon died as he looked upon her naked form.

She laid back on her elbows, breasts pushed forward, her nipples a rosy pink that peaked and begged for his mouth. Arcaeus allowed his gaze to travel lower, each of Arianna's curves admired with his eyes before they stopped at the juncture of her thighs. Arcaeus expected to see a thatch of curly hair and was taken aback to instead see a small strip down the middle, as if pointing the way to her core.

He moved forward to nudge her knees apart and brought

his eyes back to her face, gaze kept locked on hers as he crawled onto the bed. He settled his thighs between Arianna's and opened her up even more.

"Arianna, I need to be inside you." Arcaeus rested his weight upon his elbows. A gentle movement of his hips and he was brushing against her core. "I will make this as pain free as possible for you, *Theia.*"

Arianna's answering smile caused him to grin, but her next words stilled his course for a moment. "Arcaeus, I'm not a virgin. Please, hurry."

He groaned and, unable to hold back any longer, meshed his lips with hers. Arcaeus reached back along her thigh and grabbed her leg to wrap it around his waist. He used the same hand to reach between their bodies, then wrapped it around himself, rubbing the tip of his cock along the seam of her core and parting the soft folds to caress her nub. He watched as she arched her back, breasts pushed into his chest.

Arcaeus released his grip on his cock and moved his fingers to stroke and tease Arianna's entrance. He needed to prepare her, wanted her slick with need so he would cause no pain. Gods, she was so tight.

As his fingers grazed her entrance, he found her soaked, the evidence of her own arousal. A low growl left him as he pushed the digit slowly inside her. Arianna's core tightened around his finger and caused him to groan in anticipation.

Arcaeus pushed a second finger deep inside her, and with over five years' worth of need to spur him on, he started to kiss her frantically. In one swift move, Arcaeus removed his fingers and replaced them with the thick head of his shaft. He looked into her eyes and waited for her to say yes. He wanted her to need this as much as he did.

21

Oh God, why had he stopped? Arianna scraped her nails across his shoulders as she arched her hips up in the hope it would give him some small hint as to how she felt.

"Arcaeus, please... I need you. Oh God, please."

Arcaeus's face tensed as he bent his head to her right breast. He took the rose-pink bud between his teeth and tugged, then enveloped the whole nipple with his mouth.

"Oh God," Arianna hissed as his teeth bit into her sensitive nipple, then she screamed as, with one hard thrust, his cock was buried to the hilt deep inside her. Arianna's inner muscles tightened around his shaft and drew him in deeper.

Arcaeus started to thrust, slowly at first, setting a rhythm in time with the deep sucks on her nipples. Arianna knew she was panting and begging, but she couldn't help herself. The feel of him deep and full inside her, combined with the tugs on her nipples, sent her state of arousal sky high. She screamed his name as she raised her hips, heels dug into his arse as she met him thrust for thrust. She thrashed as he started to speed up, his pelvis hitting her own, her clit teased to the point it was almost too much to take.

Releasing her breast, Arcaeus moved his assault back to Arianna's mouth. His tongue battled with hers and mimicked what his cock was doing to her pussy. She moved her hands to grab his arse as he quickened his pace. All she was able to do was kiss him back and hang on for the ride as he took control. Arianna poured everything into that one kiss—all her emotions and desires.

Biting down on his lip, Arianna tugged on it and drew blood as she felt her imminent release. "Arcaeus... I'm, I'm—oh, God!"

Arianna felt him slip his hand between them. His talented fingers pinched her clit exactly how she needed it, and it worked like a charm as she came undone around him. Her body shuddered and pulsed as she threw her head back and screamed his name through the most intense orgasm of her life.

She laid beneath him in a euphoric state, her emotions floating as though in an out of body experience as she gazed up the male worshipping her with his body. His grunts were guttural and animalistic as he thrusted, replacing her agonized breaths with his own.

His face was bathed in pleasure as he thrusted once, then twice, before he growled out his own release. The tendons in his neck, shoulders and arms strained as his orgasm shot through his body. His hips jerked several times before he stilled and rested his forehead against her own, her name a prayer on his lips.

22

Sleep eluded Arcaeus, but he didn't care. This night had been the best of his life.

His body shook, which wasn't a bad thing after the third time of climaxing, and he lay with an exhausted Arianna sprawled across his chest, her luxurious hair fanned over his torso. She was heaven on earth, a gift from the gods made just for him.

Arcaeus had struggled to let her go before he knew her passion, but now he wouldn't even consider it. He had to persuade her to stay with him in this world. Either that or go with her to her time, but no matter what, he vowed he would never let her go again.

As he stroked Arianna's hair, he realised that after only a short time, he had lost his heart to this beautiful and strong female. He had loved Thalia, but it paled in comparison to what he felt for this woman. She was beyond all expectations. He would fight the gods themselves, even give up his life if he had to.

His fingers found the small, circular pendant she wore around her neck. In her sleep, it must have worked its way around to the back of her neck. He rubbed it with his thumb and found the words inscribed soothing. It was strange how, in this life, she was chosen by Aphrodite instead of Apollo.

For a warrior who fought for honour and for the gods, he had now found his purpose in life.

He would pledge his life, loyalty and honour to Arianna. He would ask her to be his, to be his wife.

Arcaeus untangled her limbs and hair from his body and slid off the bed. His fingers brushed against her cheek as he bent and pressed a brief kiss to her lips. He didn't want to leave her, wanted hours more of pleasure, but if he wanted to secure his dreams, he had to get to work.

For starters, he had to petition his god to marry Arianna and have the soul-searching gift removed.

Arcaeus no longer needed it.

He had accomplished what he set out to do: find his soul mate, no matter when or where, and bring them together. The gods had written that soul mates could never be parted. They were drawn together like opposing magnets, and that was true. If he had been told a week ago that he would find her, Arcaeus wouldn't have believed it.

He silently dressed and kept his eyes on Arianna as she slept. Every now and then, she emitted little noises. Oh, how he loved the sounds she made. Each one tugged at his heart.

Arcaeus prayed that she accepted him and agreed to be his. He still wasn't sure how she felt about him, but he hoped she would come to love him as time went on.

He grabbed the rest of his things and sat on the edge of the bed to stroke her hair. It felt as soft as it looked. He pressed a lingering kiss to her brow, stood up and forced himself to leave. He knew if he stayed any longer, he would be back in that bed.

He had a new life to start, and he had a lot of work to do to make it happen. Time was of the essence.

23

Arianna's body ached all over. Muscles she hadn't known existed were currently screaming, *What the hell were you thinking?*

Arianna sat up and clutched the sheet to her breasts as she looked around the room. She already knew Arcaeus wasn't around. His intense presence was missing, and she felt, deep down, that he wasn't close. But she knew he would be okay.

The single lily resting on his pillow also made her aware of the fact.

Arianna wandered around the room with the sheet draped around her body. Being alone gave Arianna the time she needed to do some serious thinking.

This man, this warrior, had made her happier in the past day than she had ever been, but the question that needed to be asked was, could she give up being a part of the future to stay here in this time with him?

Arianna's heart screamed out a loud, resounding yes, but her head was being logical. It reminded her again that they had only just met and knew nothing of each other. So how could she pin everything she'd hoped, dreamed and fantasized about on an ancient warrior who knew nothing about her, and from the very first moment, thought she had been his long-lost love?

Arianna tucked the sheet more securely under her arms and walked to the windows. Her hand pulled back the muslin curtain and she watched, amazed at the comings and goings of the ancient villa, while her mind raced over and over the pros and cons of the whole situation.

Arianna turned and made her way over to the chest at the other side of the bed. She guessed it held clothing and was proved right when she opened the lid. There was a length of the most beautiful material, and with a half-cocked attempt, she managed to wrap herself in it, the ends tied haphazardly at her shoulder, before she walked outside. Arianna followed her way around the side of the building and onto a path, and before long, she found herself stood in a small but beautiful garden.

Flowers in full bloom covered the area to each side of the path, their fragrance pleasant to the nose as Arianna meandered around the hedges.

She took a moment to enjoy the peace, so soothing to the turmoil she felt inside, and fingered the pendant at her neck. She wished, prayed and begged for help to decide what she should do.

"Oh, Aphrodite, what would you do? Marvellous! I'm now talking to the gods, never mind myself." Arianna sat on a bench that overlooked a small pond and watched as a fish broke the surface before it dove back into the depths. The scales glistened like small jewels every time the sun hit them.

So lost in her own reverie, she didn't realise someone was sat next to her.

"It is beautiful here, is it not, Arianna?"

Arianna screamed and jumped up so quickly she almost

arse-planted into the pond. She turned to focus on the stunning blonde that was now sat on the bench. Her eyes were intense but an unusual shade of violet, and her long hair was a shimmering mass of gold that complimented the bright red dress she wore. She stood in one graceful movement, and Arianna could only stare as she felt a combination of awe and envy. Only a goddess could be this beautiful.

"It's rude to stare, Arianna, so come take your seat again. I am sorry I disturbed you, but I did hear the wish you made on my pendant. I know you require help, and I always help my priestesses."

Arianna's mouth opened then closed, like the fish she had just watched, but nothing came out. She took a deep breath before she blurted out, "Fuck! You're Aphrodite!"

Arianna swiftly covered her mouth with her hand and looked sheepish as she faced the goddess. Their eyes met and she felt somewhat relieved when Aphrodite smiled then chuckled at her unladylike language.

"Yes," she said with a nod. "I am the goddess Aphrodite, deity to love in all its aspects. I heard you that day, Arianna. I heard your soul calling out. I could do naught but help you."

Frowning, Arianna stepped closer. "Wait, you're the one who brought me here? No!" Realisation suddenly dawned. "You pushed me down the stairs, didn't you?"

The goddess refused to meet her eyes for a second and her cheeks pinkened, before she finally looked up and answered Arianna's question. Arianna folded her arms across her chest and waited patiently.

"Yes. I may have given you a gentle nudge, but it was for your own good, and it got you here to your soul mate. I believe that is all that matters."

Arianna stepped closer and thought, not for the first time, a firm sod it. She sat down next to Aphrodite, the material of her dress clutched in her small hands. All of Arianna's worries and insecurities rushed to the forefront of her mind.

"Can you send me back?" Arianna looked up into one of the most beautiful faces she had ever seen, surprised to see Aphrodite frowning, severely.

"You want to leave, but why? I thought—well, after last night I was under the impression you wanted to be here and to be with Arcaeus."

"How do you know about last night?" Arianna's face flushed a bright red as her memories took her back to the best night of her life, to the touch of her warrior. Deciding she didn't want to know, she continued. "I have a life back home, a job and friends that would miss me. I can't just disappear. I love it here, but what if it doesn't work? What if he is like every other man I've known? What if he gets bored with me and I'm stuck here? What am I supposed to do then?"

Arianna knew full well her voice was getting higher in pitch, but she couldn't help it. She felt herself start to panic.

Her tone sharp, Aphrodite cut through her tirade. "Arianna, calm yourself this second. You will be happy here because he loves you. It's in his aura, and I have never seen it shine so brightly. You are a clever girl, and I have no doubt you can survive here, if you just open yourself to him."

Aphrodite clasped Arianna's hands between her own and looked at her with emotional violet eyes. "Trust in the warrior, Arianna. He will move heaven and earth to make you happy."

With those words, she leaned forward and placed a gentle kiss on Arianna's brow before letting go of her hands. The goddess stood and walked towards the villa, the sun shining brightly just as she vanished like she'd never been there.

She shook her head in awe, a little dumbstruck that she had just been in the presence of a goddess.

"Now that was some freaky shit, Anya." Arianna stood, only to realise her name was being called.

She smiled and found herself racing back as Arcaeus's voice boomed from the villa, calling her name. Honesty compelled her to admit to herself that she had missed him, and she felt desperate to be back in his arms.

Oh boy, Aphrodite was right. She had that deep-down gut feeling that she might actually have fallen for him.

24

Where had she gone? Arcaeus knew he sounded worried as he called Arianna's name, but he had descended into a panic when he returned home to find she had vanished.

"Arianna," Arcaeus called out again as he paced the courtyard. His servants had already scattered in a desperate dash to find their new mistress.

In his hand he clutched the small velvet bag. He felt his fingers tighten around it as he called out again. This time he stopped and listened. Was that her?

He called again. "Arianna, where are you?"

This time there was an answer.

"Arcaeus, I'm here!"

He let out a breath he hadn't realised he'd been holding as she appeared from behind one of the trees that signalled the start of the gardens.

She ran straight for him, a dazzling smile on her face, taking her from beautiful to breath-taking. Could that be for him? Had she missed him as much as he missed and craved her?

Opening his arms, he met her halfway. Swinging her up, he brought her into his chest, his face buried in her shoulder as he spun her in a circle.

"Arianna, where did you go? I was worried." He slid her down his body and placed her feet on the ground, his arms still wrapped tightly around her waist.

"Just into the gardens. I needed to think, Arcaeus."

He didn't ask what she needed to think about. He just hoped she would choose him.

Arcaeus walked her over to a bench by the bathing pool and sat her down. He knelt in front of her and, without saying a word, handed her the velvet bag and waited. He tried to keep his face blank as he watched her slowly open the bag, gently tipping it up until the tiny gold pendant held within fell into her palm.

He'd had it made by the goldsmith in the village years ago, when he was going to marry Thalia, but after being with his *Theia,* he had headed straight to the goldsmith and had it changed. This time it suited the passionate woman he had fallen in love with.

It was a simple gold disc with a small fire opal set in the centre. The fiery red gem sparkled in the sun as she turned it over. On the back, he'd had their names engraved.

"Arcaeus, this is stunning." She looked him in the eye, the pendant clutched in her fingers. "Why?" The simple question pulled him from his thoughts. He smiled.

"*Theia,* it is my gift to you, a symbol of what I feel and how I want us to be together... forever. Arianna, will you make me the happiest man alive by becoming my wife?" He watched as her eyes widened. She looked from his face and back down to the pendant.

"Arcaeus... we hardly know each other."

He stood and brought her into his embrace, his chin resting on her head. "I know all I need to, *Theia*. You are my match in every way, and I want you for eternity." He pulled back to look into her eyes. "That's if you will have me."

Arianna took a visible breath before she answered. "Let me think about this, Arcaeus. It's a lot to take in, especially if it means giving up any chance of going home."

Arcaeus didn't have a chance to answer as she meshed her lips with his. Slender arms wrapped around his neck; delicious breasts pressed into his chest.

Groaning, Arcaeus palmed her arse cheeks, picked her up and backed her into the sidewall of the villa. Hidden from view of the servants, he plundered her mouth and slid his hands over her hips to her thighs. He grabbed the material of her dress and moved it out of his way. Determined to bring her pleasure and hopefully change her mind, Arcaeus continued to kiss Arianna with a ferocity he had never felt before, whilst his hand found her already soaked core. "Bless the gods, you are so wet for me, my *Theia*. Let me ease that ache for you."

Arianna's moans gave Arcaeus all the permission he needed. The pads of his fingers gently brushed her opening, collecting her nectar before circling it around her swollen nub. Her mewls of delight sounded in his ears while her hands tugged on his hair, guiding his actions.

He kept the pad of his thumb on her nub, circling and pushing, before he inserted a finger into her core. He growled as her inner walls clenched around his digit. Her body was slick and welcoming as he inserted a second. He twisted and curled his fingers to find and press against that perfect spot that made Arianna gasp for breath.

"Come for me, my *Theia*. Let me feel and hear your release for your warrior. Your soul mate." He devoured her mouth once more and increased the pace. Her warm honey coated his hand as she erupted in his arms.

Arianna's scream of delight was muffled by his mouth as

he slowed the sensual assault. Loving the dazed look on her face, he snagged her gaze and eased his fingers from her trembling body. He brought his fingers to his mouth and sucked them clean of her release. "Mm, you taste like ambrosia."

He bent down to kiss her and set her feet to the floor. "Arianna, my *Theia*, I will go to the temple of Apollo to petition the god. I will marry you, do you understand?"

Her simple nod made him smile.

"Good, now go inside and get ready. I will return for you in two hours." Arcaeus stroked her cheek and kissed her once more. "And tonight, my love, you will be mine. In all ways."

Stepping back, he took her gently by the arm and lead her to their rooms. He couldn't help but feel elated, not only by the passion-filled, glazed look on her face but the fact she had agreed. He knew she would most likely berate him later, so he didn't mention it again.

He kept her in his sight until she was safely in their room. Then he made his way outside and whistled for his stallion, eager to get this part of his plan over with. Arcaeus vaulted onto Balios's back, giving the horse the rein. "Make haste, Balios!"

He sped off to the Temple of Apollo and, hopefully, to a god in a good mood.

25

Was she now engaged?

How in God's name had that happened? One minute, they were sat talking. The next, he had decided to propose. Arianna then found herself in his arms, overtaken by drugging kisses and an orgasm so earth shattering she had agreed to Arcaeus's request.

Her body still shook. No man had ever done that to her. He had known exactly where she wanted to be touched, and by God, he had known exactly how to as well. Arianna was still weak-kneed from her orgasm.

Either he had been desperate to get in her panties or the sneaky warrior had known she would've have agreed to anything, just as long as he kept kissing and touching her as he had done.

"Oh, he is so going to pay for that," Arianna said, with no real heat to her words

Arianna sat on the edge of the bed and looked down at the small gold pendant still clutched in her hand, the colour of the small, fiery stone a mix between orange and red. It was stunning. And surprisingly, exactly what she would have chosen for herself.

She held up the pendant and was mesmerised by the way the stone shone in the sunlight that beamed through the open windows.

"Oh, sod it!" Arianna said to herself. She seemed to be doing that a lot lately—talking to herself. She unclasped her necklace and slid her engagement gift onto the chain, the new pendant bumping against the old. She placed the chain back around her neck and felt a comfortable warmth as they both settled against her skin.

"Perfect!" Arianna got up and took some much-needed deep breaths as she thought of her warrior.

Arianna's hand flew to her mouth. *Her* warrior. It was official; she was now calling him her own. She shook her head and called out. Her call was soon answered by one of the servants, who rushed in to help Arianna get ready. She had no clue how these Chitons worked or even went on, and, honestly, she wanted to look her best.

If Arcaeus wanted to marry her, then she was going to make an effort. Another first on her part.

***

Apollo grinned as he walked away from the viewing pool. So, the brave Arcaeus was on his way here to petition for the soul-searching gift to be removed, and for him to bless a union.

Oh, he couldn't wait to see the look on the warrior's face when he was forced to come to terms with his fate and realise this had been the plan all along. Apollo snapped his fingers and called two of his slaves forward.

"Ready my chamber for our guest of honour and bring

my toys." He turned away from the slave and felt a lightness that had been distant from his being for a long time.

Finally, he would get the justice he felt he deserved. No one, and he meant no one—not even Zeus himself—would ever again make him feel the way Desma had all those years ago.

He had managed a small part of his revenge on her, but most of it would be enacted on her son.

He would suffer, and the torture would not be quick. As for the priestess, Apollo looked forward to getting his hands on her.

Apollo sat back on his dais and called for another goblet of ambrosia. Things were going swimmingly.

26

Arcaeus's heart felt light and free and so full he thought it might burst. She had said yes. Thalia—no, Arianna—was going to be his wife and life partner. He couldn't help but grin as he nudged Balios, the horse responding to the silent order and quickening his pace.

The scenery sped by as they galloped to the Temple of Apollo. The single-storey structure stood alone on a hill outside of the town, its location perfect for receiving the sun from dawn until dusk. The white marbled columns shone brightly in the midday sun, but it was the statue of the god himself that could be seen from all angles, that outshone the temple. It had been wrought from gold dug from the base of Olympus herself, and depicted the god in full glory.

Arcaeus pulled Balios to a stop at the base of the hill and slid off him, his gaze locked on the temple high above.

So, this was it. After all this time and heartache, his future was finally within his grasp. All that was left was to get the gift removed. He no longer required the ability to find souls, for the only one he had ever wanted was now his and his forever.

Arcaeus had been taught from an early age about soul mates. A person was forever blessed if they found their soul mate, and it was written and willed for by Aphrodite herself that soul mates were destined to find each other.

Arcaeus had never truly believed it, but now he had no doubts at all. He knew that no matter where, or in what time, his mate was, he would be able to find her, and she would be able to find him. They were meant to be, for it was now written.

Arcaeus started up the hill with slow, purposeful strides, the beauty of his surroundings forgotten and ignored as he climbed the steps and strode into the temple. His footsteps echoed on the marble floor as he walked through the decorated archway, the interior lit only by flaming sconces and the sun reflecting off the golden statue of Apollo.

Something didn't feel right. Arcaeus stopped in the alcove by the high altar. His training and years of battle had him instinctively reaching for the sword strapped to his hip. After a while, Arcaeus started to relax his guard. He was just being paranoid. He was so on edge about the whole situation that he half expected something to go wrong.

He stepped up to the altar and took out a knife, then calmly drew it across his palm and watched his life blood drip into the gold blessing bowl that sat in the centre.

"Blessed Apollo, I beseech thee. I offer my humble blood as tribute to your name. Please hear this mortal's plea." He knelt in front of the altar as he spoke the offering, his voice the only sound to rebound off the walls of the temple. He kept his eyes closed and prayed long and hard for the god to appear and grant him audience this one last time.

With his head tipped up, Arcaeus looked around the temple. The feeling that something was off just wouldn't go away. Curiosity got the better of him, and he headed to the back of the temple.

Where was everyone? This was one of the few temples that always teemed with people making offerings or praying.

Arcaeus stepped through the arched doorway into the back chamber, hoping to find out what was going on. A brisk wind wrapped around Arcaeus, icy in its presence. A gentle tug on the back of his neck brought about the realisation that he had stepped into a trap. A noose tightened around his neck, its origin unknown as his fingers fought the tightening cord.

"What is this?" Arcaeus's voice croaked as the cord tightened. His vision rapidly went dark as oxygen was denied to him.

Forced to his knees, Arcaeus's fingers clawed at his own neck, his lungs desperate for breath. Confused and, for once, frightened, Arcaeus saw the gold-booted feet of his god approach, along with what must be his slaves at his side.

"Well, well, well, Arcaeus. I was wondering when you were going to arrive. I'm not a patient deity." The god's laugh was wickedly evil as he reached past the warrior's shoulder to tug on the near invisible cord that continued to tighten.

"Arcaeus, what a fool you've been. Thinking you could mislead a god, especially a god like me. You see, I have known about you and my priestess all along. Why do you think I had her sacrificed?"

Arcaeus frowned in confusion. His inability to talk hindered his fight, so he listened and learned. With each word, his heart began to break.

Apollo sat next to the warrior's fallen form and told his tale. "Your mother, the whore that she was, actually had the nerve to refuse my suit. And Arcaeus, no one does that to me. The God of the Sun always gets his payback. So, you are all part of my revenge. But don't worry, I won't be sacrificing your woman again."

Arcaeus's heart stopped. The thought of what this vindictive god could do to Arianna made his blood run cold.

"Your lady—Arianna, I think she goes by now? —will be made very good use of. I have rather taken a fancy to her, especially after hearing her pleasure when you took her against the wall. I would like to see and experience that firsthand."

With a pat on the warrior's shoulder, Apollo stood and bid his slaves to pick up the nearly unconscious form of Arcaeus.

Apollo grabbed the warrior's chin and looked straight into his face. "Know this, Arcaeus. You will suffer at my hand and it will not be quick. But before you die—and I can assure you, you *will* die—you will see me take your woman. You will see and hear her cry out in pleasure as I wipe your memory from her mind and make her my own."

With those last words, Arcaeus's weak form was tied to a large wooden post, before he was dragged to the temple's back chamber. He was stripped and left in just a small cloth that covered his hips as another slave prepared a knife. He tensed as a third slave approached with the famed Scorpion Whip of the Eumenides.

Head down, Arcaeus prayed Arianna kept away, and that some other god would take pity on him and offer him a quick death.

27

"I feel sick." Arianna began to talk to herself again. She wrapped her arms around her waist. The stomach cramps seemed to have gotten worse as the hour passed. It was as though something inside her was being tugged and pulled at, even cut into.

She clutched her stomach and paced the outer dressing room. How long had it been since Arcaeus left?

Arianna looked down at herself and managed to smile through the constant pain of the stomach cramps. The warrior had chosen well. She was already in love with her chiton. It was the most beautiful turquoise colour that Arianna had ever seen, even more breath-taking than the Mediterranean Sea itself.

The servant, Amelia, had performed a miracle with Arianna's hip-length hair. She had pinned it in various places to let the natural curls frame her face, a decoration of freshwater pearls woven in and out.

Arianna stopped her pacing and perched on a stool. She rocked gently as another wave of pain, and this time nausea, flashed through her. In that instant, Arianna closed her eyes.

The vision she saw was of blood—so much blood—and what looked to be a whip.

Her eyes shot open as she heard her name being whispered, the voice one she would know anywhere as she saw dark, chocolate brown eyes overshadowed with pain.

"Arcaeus... No. No, it can't be you!" Arianna bolted to her feet, picked up her skirts and ran outside as fast as her legs would carry her. Her voice was a high-pitched shrill as she screamed the name of Arcaeus's man servant.

"Andreus!" she screamed again. She had the sickening feeling that she was too late for something. It was too deeply ingrained to shift. Arianna knew something was wrong and that something had happened to her warrior. Shit.

"Someone get me a fucking horse, damn it!"

Arianna felt tears leak from her eyes. Dread unfurled in her stomach, only to be replaced with nausea. Her feet led her to the entrance as she waited for a ride of some sort. In her rush to leave the villa's main building, she had, on impulse, grabbed a small dagger from Arcaeus's office, its hilt now clutched firmly in her palm.

Arianna's adrenaline shot sparks through her blood as a small mare was led to the mounting block.

Shocked etched across Arianna's face as she watched Cosmos walk alongside Andreus, her mare and his own stallion following close behind. His face was all harsh lines and seriousness. "My lady, I already know I cannot keep you from following Arcaeus, but please allow me to accompany you. Arcaeus would gut me where I stand if I did not protect you in his stead."

Arianna nodded and turned. Without waiting for the servant to saddle the mare, she lifted her skirt and slid her leg over the horse's back. Arianna grabbed the mane, and with a swift kick to the mare's flanks, urged her into a gallop.

She went with the feeling that things had gone terribly

wrong and rushed in the direction of what she hoped was Apollo's temple. The presence of Cosmos almost soothed her frayed nerves. At least she knew they wouldn't get lost.

She prayed to Aphrodite herself that her gut was wrong, and that she wasn't too late.

Riding in a dress was something Arianna would not recommend. Her thighs were on fire, yet she ignored the pain and rode on. The road itself wound through the fields and in any other situation Arianna would have enjoyed the freedom of riding, with the breeze in her hair and the sun on her face. Yet without Arcaeus by her side it meant nothing.

The deep-seated feeling of anxiety within her increased as they rounded the last bend near the temple to find it blocked by four soldiers. Arianna winced when she recognised the one who had struck her. His smile when he saw her was one that sent chills through her blood.

"Oh look, the whore is back," he shouted as she brought her horse to a stop. Cosmos rode past her, his sword already drawn and a war cry on his lips as he engaged the soldiers. Their own swords were slow to emerge as they fumbled to protect themselves from the warrior. Arianna fought to keep her seat on her horse as the men battled.

"My lady," Cosmos shouted over the din as metal struck metal. He had already taken out two of the four soldiers and now battled the one who had taken a dislike to her. "Go... Go now. I will be right behind you."

Arianna nodded and kicked her horse into action. The small beast bucked before it moved forward, knocking over a soldier that was trying to get to his feet. Her horse quickly moved to a canter as she flew up the road, that feeling of anxiety only growing inside her.

28

Fire and pain. So much pain.

Arcaeus blinked back into consciousness. Being whipped wasn't the worst part of the torture that Apollo dished out. The main problem came from the poison that accompanied the Scorpion Whip.

A small whip, not something that looked intimidating, that had three leather lengths to it. Each tip held a barb from a scorpion, and each, to his now personal knowledge, was laced with venom.

The venom, once in the bloodstream, burned like liquid fire and caused the warrior to convulse, even as they continued to whip him. Arcaeus had lost count of how many times he had sunk into the abyss, but every time he had come around to the smirking face of Apollo, who sat on a golden throne, in pride of place, as if it were something he watched every day.

A scream was wrenched from the warrior's lips as the slave delivered the last blow of the whip, slicing him to the bone. This time its barbs dug in and removed strips of flesh as it was ripped away. Sagging against the wooden post,

Arcaeus fought to fill his lungs as the tremors started, each breath agony, as the latest wave of venom flowed like a raging river through his body. Sweat coated his torso like a fine mist.

His reprieve was short lived as a slave grabbed his hair and yanked his head back. He was forced to stand as another approached with a heated knife, its blade glowing as red as fresh blood, the heat palpable. A handful of flesh was grabbed from the warrior's lower back and stretched out—before the blade cut through Arcaeus's skin and muscle. His flesh sizzled, the heat cauterizing the wound immediately.

Arcaeus couldn't hold back his scream of pain. As he used what was left of his strength, he thrashed against the wooden post. The ropes cut and sliced into his wrists, and blood slowly seeped down his arms, the bright red droplets soon forming streams as gravity took hold.

Out of the corner of his eye, as blurry as his sight was, he made out the god on his dais. The bastard had a huge grin plastered across his face as he watched his slave slice into the warrior's skin. Arcaeus couldn't focus anymore. The pain overwhelmed him, to the point he was regularly passing out. The full weight of his body suspended from his wrists caused the skin and tendons to be crushed and torn.

His body was exhausted, not only from the beating, but also from the loss of blood. He couldn't remember how long he had been hanging from the post. He was awakened after the last session of torture by repeated punches to the face.

Arcaeus growled at the slave and tried to pull himself up on the post, if only to reduce the tension on his now battered and bleeding wrists. He was turned around to face Apollo. His anger erupted in full force as the god just grinned.

"Why?" he shouted, his voice harsh and raw from screaming. "Tell me why. What have I ever done for you to hate me so? I have spent my entire life serving you!" The speech quickly delivered, he sagged again. Arcaeus gritted his teeth against the agony as his naked and sliced flesh connected with the wood.

"Why, you ask me?" The god laughed as he got up to walk over to the warrior, the evil glint in his eye unnerving as he snatched the Scorpion Whip out of the slave's hand. He flexed it, tested its weight.

"I will tell you why, Arcaeus, so as you die, you will know a god's pain." A smirk on the god's face, he swung the whip. The fronds lashed across the warrior's chest, eliciting another scream from Arcaeus, as well as a chunk of his flesh.

"Your mother, Arcaeus... Your mother was my favourite priestess. She was mine. She belonged to me! I gave her everything, and what did she do?" He brought his face inches from Arcaeus's and continued to shout. "She petitioned me for a blessing—a blessing to leave my temple and get married. She snubbed a god to be with a mortal, and then she produced you. So you, Arcaeus, are paying for your mother's sins. You are very much like your mother, as you proved five years ago when you attempted to take one of my priestess's away." The god laughed; a cruel sound that sent a shiver up the warrior's spine.

"You actually thought you could keep that a secret." Apollo leaned down to whisper in Arcaeus's ear. "You know that's why she was sacrificed, don't you? Because of you."

Arcaeus's scream of rage echoed around the temple as he thrashed and tried to get to the god, to wrap his hands around his throat and watch as the life left his eyes.

Apollo smirked and grasped the warrior's chin. He held it firmly as he looked him straight in the eye.

"Pity you didn't see Thalia's sacrifice." The cruelty etched on the god's face made Arcaeus sick. "You see, before I slit her throat, I made her scream."

Another whispered sentence from the god caused

Arcaeus to buck against the post in fury. "She screamed your name, Arcaeus, as I took her on the floor of my temple, spilling her blood as I spilled my seed."

The god laughed and threw the whip back to his slave, before turning his back on the Arcaeus.

"Continue the whipping. Leave no skin untouched!"

29

Arianna's heart pounded as she stood in a shadowed alcove of the temple. She placed a hand over her mouth and silently listened to Apollo torment and torture Arcaeus, feeling the slow track of tears again rolling down her cheeks. The confession of Apollo's plan and of what he did to Thalia was monstrous.

Arianna's race to the temple had not been easy. The mare hadn't liked being rushed and even had the nerve to buck Arianna off her back.

Her beautiful dress was now ripped down the side. She had leaves in her hair, mud streaked across her face, and what little patience she'd had to begin with had all but disappeared.

Arianna dragged her concentration back to the present and shivered as Apollo boasted his pleasure of not only raping Thalia, but ending her life, his harshly delivered words sadistic and cruel.

The low sound of footsteps caused Arianna to tense. Apollo and his following words made her blood run cold. "Continue the whipping. Leave no skin untouched!"

Hell no! Not on her watch.

Arianna bent down and grabbed the dagger she had secured to her ankle, its weight unfamiliar but comfortable in her palm. Her anger started to swell as the sounds of whipping echoed loudly, soon followed by the harsh groans of pain from Arcaeus, his tone so broken she knew he had been screaming for a long time.

Arianna peeked around the corner and was presented with the back of Apollo's dais. His fingers tapped on the armrest in time with every crack of the whip. His nonchalance as he sat and enjoyed the show made Arianna retch as the bile in her stomach rose.

The hilt of the dagger bit into Arianna's palm as she gripped it tighter.

She let her eyes roam over the scene and made a mental note of the slaves and their positions, as well as the god himself.

What are you doing, Arianna? You aren't a fighter. The logical side of her brain screamed and begged her to run, but her heart was in full control, and it constricted as Arianna's eyes came to rest on the battered body of her warrior.

His arms were pulled up straight, above his head, the ropes tied around his wrists ripping into his skin every time his body jerked with the contact of the whip. Streams of blood flowed down his body, not only from the cuts on his wrists but the deep welts from the whip, and... oh God, they had been cutting chunks of flesh from his body.

A loud sob escaped her mouth and brought with it the attention of the slaves and Apollo.

She gripped the dagger and stepped fully into the chamber, her gaze locked on Arcaeus. She ignored the others in the room as her feet took her swiftly to her warrior's side.

"Arcaeus, what have they done to you?" Arianna whispered to her warrior as she gently took his face in her hands and turned his unconscious form toward her own body. Her lips brushed across his blood-soaked ones, and she let out another sob. She felt her heart breaking with every breath. This strong, virile warrior had been reduced to this because of one arrogant being's pride.

Arianna stroked her warrior's cheek, took a deep breath, and turned to face the arsehole responsible.

"Arianna, is it? I was wondering when you were going to arrive." The god stood and walked toward her, his gait long and swift.

Arianna placed herself between Arcaeus and the god, not sure what she could do but determined to not let anything else happen to him.

"Why the hell have you done this? What is your goddamn problem?" Arianna lifted her chin and looked the god square in the eye. Inside, she was absolutely petrified, but, if she was honest, she no longer gave a shit. The one man who had finally made her feel wanted, who liked her for being herself, was now hanging onto his life by a thread.

"You fucking coward! Feel good, do you, torturing a man because his mother didn't want you? And who could blame her? You are a prick! No woman would want a man who loves himself more than he could love her." The words were shouted into the god's face as Arianna reached her hand back to touch Arcaeus. Just his presence, even unconscious, gave her strength.

The god's face morphed as she shouted at him. Gone was the smirk, and in its place was a mask of pure fury.

"Silly mortal to berate a god. I think it's time we changed the game and played with *you*." His hand shot out and grabbed Arianna by the throat. He jerked her off her feet and close to him, her grip on her warrior ripping free.

"Let's see what happens when you remember your past,

little priestess." His words barely registered before blackness consumed Arianna.

Like a movie being played, Arianna watched as a multitude of scenes were shown to her. She quickly realised that the 'movie' was about Thalia's' life, or Arianna's past. Whichever was the truth.

It all started when she pledged her loyalty to Apollo. Her devotion to the god was her only aim in life, to serve. Her life flashed past quickly; the day she met Arcaeus, how he had shown her kindness and respect. Her warrior had courted her, showered her with love, true love like nothing she had felt before. Arianna's vision showed how their love had grown from a small spark into a raging fire of pure and undiluted love. She remembered clearly the day she had been marked, how she had been unable to stop crying and had felt her heart break in two when she faced her warrior and told him she had to leave him. Her heartbeat tripled at the memory of the day she died, as well as the assaults to her. They were replayed over and over again. Arianna's heart hammered as she was brought back to the present. Her blood boiled with anger as she slowly opened her eyes and stared straight at the god.

Arianna lifted the dagger and sliced it into the arm that held her neck. The sharp and sudden pain caused the god to drop her.

"You will not touch us!" Arianna shouted. Her voice sounded strange as her past life and consciousness began to merge with the present. Thalia and Arianna became one, and expectedly, not too happy with the wanker who stood a few metres in front of them.

"Arianna." The harsh, strangled whisper from behind had Arianna spinning around. She bolted straight to Arcaeus's side, slashed at the ropes with her dagger, and tried to hold his weight as he sank to the floor, his strength totally depleted.

"Shh, Arcaeus, don't move. You are going to be fine." Arianna stroked his cheek as she looked into pain-filled eyes that called to her and always had throughout the ages.

The sounds of battle, metal on metal, could be heard from outside the temple, the familiar voice of Cosmos and his war cry echoing. Yet Arianna ignored it. The only thing that mattered now was the man in her arms. He would always be the only thing that mattered to her. He was her heart and her soul.

30

Arcaeus's hand shook as he reached up to stroke Arianna's cheek. He looked into her eyes.

"Arianna... my *Theia*. I love you, but you must go. It's not safe... Don't want you... hurt." His voice broke as she laid him down on the floor. His head placed down carefully, Arianna got up and again faced the god.

"Heal him!" she screamed.

The god laughed in her face, its sound cruel and harsh as he uttered one word: "No."

He raised his hand, and the dagger flew from her grasp. Her scream of outrage echoed across the temple as she stood tall, her chin raised as she portrayed open defiance.

"Go on then. Do it! "Arianna shouted again. Arcaeus attempted to move as he tried to protect her.

"I don't intend to kill you, Arianna. I can hurt you in better and in much more enjoyable ways. But first, let us be rid of the company." With those words, the dagger flew past her head and into the chest of her warrior, who had used the last of his strength to stand and come to her rescue.

The dagger hit with precision and such force it embedded to the hilt.

"No!" Arianna screamed as she turned and ran to Arcaeus's side, his wide-eyed expression so painful as he looked at the dagger, then to her, before he collapsed to the ground. Apollo's laugh of pleasure went ignored as she scooped Arcaeus's head into her lap.

"Arcaeus, stay awake. Stay with me. Please, I need you!"

His hand weak, Arcaeus raised it to cup Arianna's cheek.

"Arianna... I found you, my love... My *Theia*. I will..." his voice tapered off as blood ran from his mouth, "always find... you." His hand dropped to her neck and touched the pendants resting there before it fell to the floor.

"Call... Aphrodite." His whispered breath was the last thing Arianna heard before the light in his eyes dimmed and blinked out.

"No. No, don't you dare! Arcaeus, no... I love you, dammit. Come back!" Arianna felt her heart break in two as her hand rested on her warrior's chest. There was no warmth, no heartbeat.

Arcaeus, the man from her dreams, was gone.

Dead.

Apollo watched the priestess. Her sobs heightened his pleasure as the warrior took his last breath.

Finally, his revenge was all but complete. Now he could have some real fun with this luscious female. He stalked towards the still form of Arcaeus and watched as the priestess's hands tugged and pushed at his form. He couldn't help but smile as she whispered her feelings and begged him to wake up.

"Come, priestess! He has departed." Apollo held out his

hand and watched her bowed head, her slumped shoulders. She wouldn't dare deny him. After all, she belonged to him, and she was in his temple.

"Fuck you!" The harsh reply shocked him as he dropped his hand and was met with angry green eyes that sparked with fury. "Don't you dare come anywhere near me, you selfish bastard."

He watched again as she stroked the warrior's hair. Her other hand gripped his shoulder as if she were willing him to return.

Anger at her attitude swelled within him and turned his usual, beautiful countenance into a fierce scowl. His voice boomed throughout the temple. "Do not speak to me in such a way, you pitiful, mortal bitch."

He grasped the female's hair and tugged her tear-streaked face upwards, so her eyes could meet his. "You are mine, Arianna, and have been since the day you pledged your blessing. You cannot escape, and I will do what I want. But please scream as loud as you like. No one will hear you, but I enjoy the sound." He pulled harder on her hair to give his demand more emphasis and dragged her away from the warrior's lifeless body.

"No!" she screamed. She fought with her hands, scratching and clawing at him, but was unable to hold on to Arcaeus. The sound alone brought joy to Apollo's ears. This is what he had planned; to make Arcaeus suffer and to have this fiery morsel do his bidding. He released her hair and slowly circled her sobbing form, his eyes roving over her voluptuous body. He let his mind wander and form exquisite fantasies. She may fight it now, but she would come to enjoy his attentions.

Apollo stopped just in front of her and listened. Too busy in thought of the possibilities to come, he missed her whispered words.

"What did you say, priestess?"

Apollo watched as Arianna lifted her head, her eyes still full of tears but also holding defiance as her voice lifted and filled the temple. "Aphrodite, hear my call. I bid you help *your* priestess! My heart is true, my soul lost. I need you, my goddess. Blessed be."

He watched in shock as she produced the dagger that had been embedded in Arcaeus's chest and swiped it across her palm, forming a deep gash. The blood flowed quickly as she formed a fist.

"Aphrodite, I offer my blood as a token of my love and trust." Her final plea filled the chamber.

"What have you done, you foolish girl? No other god may enter here without my permission!" He laughed as she held out her palm. A slave to gravity, the blood dripped to the marble floor

"You cannot escape your fate!" His words loud and final, he grabbed her hair and started to drag her toward the prepared chambers at the rear.

"Now stop this foolishness. It's time to start the pleasantries."

31

Oh God, no!

Her thoughts raced, her mind in so much turmoil she was almost ready to pass out.

Her warrior was dead, her goddess hadn't answered her desperate prayers, and now this monster of a god was about to repeat what he did to her in a former life. Arianna felt her heart hammer against her chest, and she started to shake.

She scratched and clawed at the hand that held her hair, fought with all her might to get loose. Fear, pure and simple, took a firm grip, and she felt the first sign of defeat as she realised there was nothing she could do to stop him.

"Stop!"

Arianna's head burned from the constant tug on her scalp, the tears long gone, as though she had nothing left to give. The sobs eventually turned to dry heaving. Arianna's mind took longer than usual understand what was happening around her.

"Apollo, I suggest you remove your hands from my priestess before I get really angry." Aphrodite's growl of displeasure made Arianna's heart soar with relief. And that feeling was only heightened as her unexpected presence caused Apollo to release her from his grip.

"Your priestess? I think not, my sister. Now be a good girl and get out of my temple. I have things to do." Before Apollo was able to grab her hair or any other part of her again, Arianna scurried, on hands and knees, out of the way; to hide herself beside a column as she watched the two deities face off.

The goddess, hip leaning against a table, checked her nails as though already bored with the conversation.

"Yes, brother, my priestess. This incarnation pledged her loyalty to me back in her time. To be honest, I thought you would have noticed. But I forgot just how much your head is full of your own importance. It makes me fearful for the sanity of your future offspring." Her sickly-sweet smile gave her words more potency.

"Sister, you overstep your boundaries, and you have obviously been hanging around the mortals for far too long. Now leave, before I get really angry." Apollo's voice was harsh and angry, and Arianna's body started to quake. She looked around the room, her eyes settling once more on Arcaeus. His body was so still. The pool of blood surrounding his form was already starting to congeal. Arianna broke into sobs again as she crawled to him.

How had this man become her world in such a short period of time? She already missed his voice, his eyes, and the aura of strength he'd projected. Arianna had never felt as safe with anybody else. She had been willing and desperate to be with him, even sacrificed going home to her own time, happy, though admittedly nervous, to be a warrior's wife and live in a time that was worlds apart from her own.

She lifted Arcaeus's head, gently placing it into her lap, and watched the gods. Aphrodite, a vision in red, stood and watched her brother as he paced the chamber. Each step only seemed to make him angrier.

"You annoy me, sister." Apollo waved his hand in the air and ignored her as he stalked towards Arianna, his jaw set as he reached out to grab her shoulder.

"Apollo, I said stop, and I meant it. Touch her again and you will regret it." Aphrodite's words caused Apollo's eye to twitch. He ignored his sister and grabbed Arianna's shoulder.

His fingers dug into her soft flesh, and he started to pull at her. Arcaeus's head lolled to the side as it slipped from Arianna's lap. The thud as his skull made contact with the floor triggered Arianna's temper to flare. Her glare connected with his conceited grin.

"You heard her, arsehole, get off me!" The previous events had taken their toll, and Arianna felt herself lose it.

She ripped his hand off her shoulder and pushed him away, her heart beating at a frantic pace as she stood. A strange burning sensation started in Arianna's stomach that travelled to her toes and fingertips. Her anger itself started to burn brighter.

She looked down at her hands, surprised to see them glow. In fact, the light covered her whole body. Another deep breath and Arianna lifted her face to look at Apollo, her anger now in full control. Arianna wasn't sure what was happening, but she didn't care.

"You ruined my future. You took away the only thing that really mattered!" Her hands glowed brighter as Arianna approached the shocked god. His eyes widened, and he stepped back tentatively as he looked from Aphrodite to Arianna.

"What?" His question was whispered as he looked to the goddess for an answer.

Her footsteps light, she walked over to take a stand behind her priestess. Aphrodite's hand lightly touched Arianna's arm before she spoke, her voice calm. "Apollo, I did warn you. You see, Arianna is pure of heart and soul, and in killing her man, as well as the wrongs you performed in her previous life... Well, I saw fit to make her blessed by a goddess, and that, dear brother, comes with its advantages."

Aphrodite's words triggered Arianna's instinct, and she stepped out from behind Aphrodite. She brought her hands up, palms out, and thrust them forward as every feeling and emotion spilled out. A bright gold light spiralled outwards, immersing the room in its glow as it headed straight for the god.

The beam nailed him in the chest and hurtled him back, into the marble wall. The building shook with the force. The only sound was Arianna's scream, and then harsh pants as she tried to catch her breath.

Arianna felt a warm hand on her shoulder as she looked through the dust to see where the god was, only to find nothing. It's was as if he had never been there. The only sign was a glaze of gold across the marble.

32

"Did I kill him?" The question echoed throughout the chamber as Arianna stood, shock flooding her system at what had just happened. The gentle touch of the goddess's hand on her shoulder offered little comfort as Arianna finally broke down. Her body shook excessively as more tears slid down her cheeks.

"No, my dear, you didn't. As a god, he is awfully hard to kill. I don't think Daddy would be too happy right now if you had killed him. But you did send my brother running with his tail between his legs."

Arianna turned to face Aphrodite, a frown pulling at her brow and her voice shaky. "What happened? Oh God, Arcaeus!"

She rushed to the warrior's side. His body laid still and stone cold. She felt her heart break all over again. She couldn't go on without him. Too many emotions swamped her as she fell to her knees and laid her head on his chest, her cries the only sound around.

"Let it all out, sweetheart. Let it out." The goddess's voice was warm and calm as she sat next to Arianna and gently rubbed her back, waiting for the cries to quieten.

"Arianna, listen. Let me tell you what happened." Arianna felt herself calm as she listened to the goddess's voice. Her eyes closed as she concentrated on the words being said.

"My little priestess, you are so much stronger than you think. The gift you were blessed with when you were born is unconditional love. Your heart and soul are pure, and it shines from within. Apollo, in his selfishness, couldn't see that, and as a male he didn't realise what breaking your heart could do. You heart is, and always will be, your weapon."

Aphrodite stroked Arianna's cheek and, hands on her arms, pulled her to stand. "Come, little one. Let us give your male a dignified send-off."

With her palms face up, Arianna watched as the goddess stood over Arcaeus. His body shimmered, and in one swift movement, the almost translucent form of Arcaeus stood up. Ghostlike in appearance, wounds healed, she instinctively knew she was seeing his soul.

Arianna felt more tears pour from her eyes as she watched the man who owned her heart entirely, turn and smile. She choked on a sob as he bowed, then winked.

"Until we meet in Elyssia, my love."

He turned and walked toward a doorway of shining light; a beautiful meadow spread beyond it. Arianna moved to follow, but a hand on her arm, belonging to the goddess, halted her progress. More sobs escaped Arianna as she watched Arcaeus's form drift out of view, then as the magical doorway closed.

At that moment, Cosmos flew into the room, seeing the last sight of his friend as he vanished into Elyssia. He fell to his knees. "I am too late. I failed you, my friend."

Aphrodite smiled at Arianna before she approached Cosmos. Her head bowed, she whispered into his ear.

Cosmos' shoulders sagged as he listened to the goddess, before he nodded, then stood. With one last look in Arianna's direction, he bowed his head and left the room.

As the goddess returned to her side, Arianna swallowed and then turned to Aphrodite, her voice barely recognisable as she asked, "What now, goddess? What am I to do?"

Arianna's heart ached, and if she was honest, all she wanted was to go home, get settled back in her own time and deal with this in a more modern way. She lifted her eyes to meet those of the goddess, hers full of understanding.

"Aphrodite, please send me home—to my time." Arianna's breath hitched on a broken sob. "Will I remember this? Will I remember Arcaeus?"

"Of course, Arianna. If that is what you want?"

Arianna clasped the pendants at her neck and nodded. "Yes, I want that. I never want to forget him."

"So be it, Arianna, but remember, should you ever need me, hold your pendant and call." With a soft smile, Aphrodite enfolded Arianna into her embrace.

"And please make sure you have some of those chocolate eggs. They are divine." Aphrodite's smile warmed her a little.

Arianna watched as Aphrodite bent to kiss her forehead. She felt the familiar fire consume her body before she descended once more.

Aphrodite looked at the unconscious form of her priestess. The dark circles under her eyes showed how exhausted she must be, and how much strain she was under. Arianna needed time to heal, and the best place to start was her temple. It also solved the question of where to send Arianna back to. She wanted to send her back to where she had been when she fell.

Apollo had gotten off lucky, and she was sorely tempted to go straight up to Olympus and turn her brother into a gorgon or something just as ugly. What was it with men lately?

She shook her head and checked her temple again to make sure Arianna would be safe until she woke or was found. Hopefully, being back in her own time would help Arianna recover from the heartbreak of watching her man die.

Crossing to the altar, Aphrodite looked at the recent offerings. The voice of her companion filled the room. "My lady, you called for me?"

Smiling, she faced the golden eagle.

"Meton. Right on time. I would ask a favour of you. Please be honest with me." She used her sweetest smile and waited for her companion to acknowledge her request.

He tilted his head as he watched her, letting her know she could hide nothing from him.

"My lady." His simple answer made her smile falter.

"Meton, my dear, do you think I'm doing the right thing?"

"Yes, Goddess, I believe in you. My belief in you has never faltered, even after all these years."

Blowing out an unladylike puff of air, she continued, "I just want to be sure. There is so much riding on this. The God of the Underworld is not affected by troubles of the heart. We must tread carefully."

Meton's golden gaze fell on her, and he said, "Am I to be privy to your plans with the other warrior, Goddess?"

Aphrodite smiled sadly. "The warrior Cosmos is aware of his fate. He knows what is needed of him, and where that could possibly lead. He's chosen friendship and loyalty over his own life. The mark of a true warrior. Let us hope he understands his burden and has the strength to see it through."

Aphrodite waved a graceful hand in front of her, and a portal appeared. On the other side was a pathway edged with starlight blooms, and the wagging tail of a three-headed dog greeted her. "Let us be gone. There is a lot of work still left for us to do."

33

"Arianna. Arianna! Wake up, sweetie. Come on, you need to wake up."

Arianna's head pounded, and the natter in her ear to wake up was not helping. She groaned and opened her eyes to the worried face of Sonia. The slow, steady beep of a machine and the quiet whispers of numerous people were the only sounds. The white walls of the room were severe and made her head pound even more. She felt confused and out of sync, with no clue as to where she was.

She looked up into the worried face of her best friend. "Sonia?"

"Oh, thank God you are okay." Sonia threw her arms around her in a tight, bruising hug. Her quiet whisper of, "I thought I had lost you," made Arianna smile.

"I'm okay, Sonia. I just have a headache." The lie passed easily through her lips. Only her head and heart knew what really happened. But she was unable to say anything, convinced she would be locked in the looney bin if she did.

"Sonia, what happened?" Arianna spoke quietly as she

leaned back against the pillows and adjusted her position in the bed. Sonia's face was a little red as she turned and helped Arianna get comfortable.

"Listen, I'm really sorry about setting up that date. I should have known he wasn't for you. I just didn't expect him to be that rude." Her face was full of remorse as she continued, "And I'm so sorry I didn't come after you when you left the restaurant. I just assumed you had gone straight home. Jesus, Anya, what made you go to the ruins? When I got back to the apartment, I totally freaked."

Sonia gripped Arianna's hands in hers and clutched them hard as she described how she had sent out a search party, only to find Arianna sprawled at the bottom of the steps of the Temple of Aphrodite. The blow to her temple had knocked her out for over a day and a half. It left the staff and her friends worried that she had slipped into a coma.

Smiling a little, she squeezed Sonia's hands back. "I'm okay, Sonia, honest. And you're right; I shouldn't have gone walking. But Andrew made me so angry that I couldn't settle."

Sonia answered her best friend with a watery smile, her happiness obvious as she followed it up with a hug that overwhelmed them both. "Okay, Anya, it's time we left this place. Hospitals give me the creeps. Let's get you back to our apartment and settled."

Arianna smiled back in the hope that she could keep this false mask in place long enough for her to find some time alone, during which she could break down. Inside, she was broken, her heart just an empty shell. Arianna closed her eyes and pictured Arcaeus. Her last happy memory was of her in his arms as she accepted his offer of marriage. Her eyes snapped open and she reached up to grab her pendants.

They sat at her throat, proof that everything was not a dream.

And then Sonia started nattering again, hurtling Arianna back into her painful reality.

34

The Underworld

Arcaeus hacked his way through the throngs of angry souls, their astral arms clawing at him. If he had been alive, his whole body, and that of his friend, Cosmos, would be in shreds by now.

He still wasn't exactly sure what had happened to get him to this point. He remembered that he had entered the Fields of Elyssia, and that he had been anxious to see his mother and father again. But his heart had also called out for his love. His Arianna.

Then Cosmos had arrived and placed a hand upon his shoulder.

He found himself faced with Hades, and everything from then on happened in a blur. But the one thing that had been definite was his overwhelming love for Arianna. Even dying wouldn't keep him from her.

So, a deal was struck.

If he and Cosmos could defeat the demons of Tartarus and cage them, as well as battle through the Fields of Punishment, they would be granted freedom from the Underworld. Both tasks would be difficult, but Arcaeus had to keep the faith; faith that he would be with Arianna again.

The Fields of Punishment housed the souls that had committed unspeakable acts, and thus were banished to suffer eternally for their crimes.

Arcaeus continued to hope, even as another wave of souls assaulted them, their putrid breath making both he and Cosmos gag.

"You had better be right, Arcaeus. If I've trusted that god and we don't find a way out, I will, in the words of Arianna, kick your arse."

Arcaeus laughed as he decapitated the head from another soul. "Cosmos, you may kick my arse all you want, but trust me when I say nothing is keeping me from getting out of here and back to my woman."

They battled hard, both covered in mud and ash, their sword skills unmatched by any in the Underworld. The exit lay not far from his view over the throngs of souls, so with more determination, they upped the pace. The flash of swords glinted in the firelight, and the limbs and bodies of the damned were quick to fall to the wayside.

Hades reached for a glass of ambrosia and offered one to the goddess sat next to him. He usually avoided the company of other gods and goddesses, but this had seemed a good reason to break that tradition, and it broke up the day for him. Sometimes even the gods got bored.

"So, Aphrodite, are you going to elaborate on why I have

two men battling their way through the Fields of Punishment?" He watched and waited for her to answer as he took a sip from the glass.

"No, Hades, I won't. But let's just say love is at work." She leaned forward and grinned as she watched the two warriors demonstrate their impressive skills with a blade.

"My dear Hades, would you like to make this a little more interesting?" She sat back in her chair and grinned. "A wager, perhaps?"

Hades sat up straighter, his eyes fixed on the warriors. "Marvellous idea, Aphrodite, and what spoils go to the winner?"

Aphrodite stood in a graceful movement, her steps fluid as she walked over to the edge of the balcony; a balcony that was only a small part of the extensive palace that made up the home of Hades.

She placed her hands upon the ornate railings and peered down. Her eyes swept across the whole of the Underworld, before her gaze finally settled upon her two warriors battling against the souls on the Fields of Punishment.

"When I win, Hades, I require the use of Cerberus, your three-headed hell hound. I want him at my disposal for a short while." She turned and faced Hades, leaning back against the railing. "What does the Lord of the Underworld require as his prize?"

Hades moved from his seat to stand next to Aphrodite and took in the view of his home. He was silent and almost brooding before he gave a curt answer.

"I require one of your love spells, Aphrodite." He gripped the railing before he smirked. "Yes, one of your love potions would suffice."

"Then a deal is struck, Hades. Now, let us watch as my warriors succeed."

Both god and goddess nodded their approval and turned

to watch the battle. Aphrodite clasped her hands together in hope that Arcaeus and Cosmos would be victorious. The cost, a love potion, wasn't what fazed her. It was the chance that Arcaeus could lose, and her plan to reunite both he and Arianna would be in jeopardy.

Cosmos could see the exit, a doorway that shimmered as if a wall of water beckoned him.

"Arcaeus, we are nearly there," Cosmos shouted, his sword arm not stopping as he decapitated yet another soul. Its translucent body screeched as shimmered then vanished. The Fields of Punishment were exactly how he imagined they would be: fields, burnt and decaying. They absorbed every negative thought from each soul trapped within its limits. He felt both physically and mentally exhausted, but he steeled himself against those emotions and ploughed on. They could rest once they had won, and their victory was close.

Head down, Cosmos battled on. His sword became an extension of himself.

We can do this. We can do this. He kept the mantra going in his head.

A brief glance up, and Cosmos was there. They had done it. They had defeated the souls on the Fields of Punishment. He turned to congratulate Arcaeus, but his eyes widened with shock as his friend became overrun, his own astral form unable to defeat the dozens of souls that clambered onto him, pulling his sword from his hand and dragging him down, their sharp teeth creating astral wounds in his body. He was overwhelmed as they attacked en masse and with more ferocity than shown before. It was as though they refused to give up one of their own. Cosmos watched as his friend vanished beneath the mass of souls, his roar of anguish echoing throughout the Underworld.

Cosmos moved to assist Arcaeus, but his feet were locked in place.

"No. Arcaeus, no! I need to help him. Don't do this!" Cosmos screamed to the gods. Aphrodite had told him he had a chance to free his friend and he had taken it. But he would rather die than leave his friend.

"No, let me help him," he screamed again.

Cosmos kept his eyes locked on his friend's plight, even as he was tugged into a blinding light, his body removed from the Underworld. Cosmos had won, but Arcaeus, for the second time, had lost. Cosmos cried out as darkness took him. No one had won but the gods.

"So, Aphrodite, it looks as though I have won," Hades said with a smile. "I believe you owe me one love potion."

Aphrodite sighed. This was not going as she had hoped. "True, Hades, both warriors didn't win, but one did. I will still honour our bargain." She turned and faced the God of the Underworld and held up a hand to stop his words. "Cosmos won, even though Arcaeus didn't. For that, I want a boon. I want Arcaeus to drink from the river Lethe. Do we have a deal?"

Hades watched the goddess and realised the fate of these two mortals meant a great deal to her. She wanted the warrior Arcaeus to drink from the river Lethe and have his soul reborn. That alone proved she was involved. He had heard rumours of her going against her brother for the sake of a mortal female and this Arcaeus. He wasn't one to meddle in the lives of mortals.

With a small bow, he answered, "Of course, Aphrodite. That is a reasonable request. It shall be done. And now for my prize." The God of the Underworld held out his hand and looked at the goddess. Aphrodite sighed and nodded in return. She clicked her fingers and a small crystal bottle that housed a shimmering red liquid appeared in Hades' palm.

"As promised, Hades. Just... use it wisely. Now, if you'll excuse me, I must go." With a flick of her wrist, Aphrodite vanished. Hades grinned at the bottle and walked back into the palace. He called for his servants to make Aphrodite's wish on the fate of her warrior happen. He had his own plans to arrange.

35

Manchester. Three months later.

"Are you kidding me? No, Susan, that does not belong there." Arianna sighed in frustration as she walked back over to the trainee. Her own irritation showed clearly as the student once again demonstrated how not to listen to a word she said.

"This jar, Susan—this is a canopic jar and it belongs in the Ancient Egyptian Exhibit, not the Ancient Greek one." Arianna placed the jar back in its protective crate and handed it over. With a forced smile, she watched the student scuttle away then turned and reached for her clipboard.

These past three months had been hell. Although, with regards to Arianna's career, it had been wonderful. They had made some fantastic finds in Greece, and the new exhibit was due to open in a week. Her main problem came when she wasn't at work. Her mind, as always, drifted to what could have been, the what ifs.

And honestly, she missed him. They may not have been together for long, but he had filled a void in Arianna's heart and soul that she felt would never be filled again. And the pendant... well, she never took it off. It was the only thing she had left of him.

Arianna reached up and touched the pendants at her neck. It had become a regular routine now. Whenever she felt like life was getting too much, she would finger the raised letters on Aphrodite's pendant, and Arianna knew that the goddess, her goddess, kept watch.

She shook herself in a bid to rid herself of the depressive thoughts and walked back to the exhibit. Arianna picked up her favourite pen and started to go over the list of items that would be needed, working out where everything would go. This had to be perfect. That was her internal mantra.

"Arianna. Hey, Arianna, where are you?" Sonia's voice echoed in the large room. Arianna was instantly suspicious. Sonia never used her full name unless she wanted something.

"I'm over by the statues, Sonia." Arianna's voice sounded harsh. She felt her mood take a downward turn. Her friend knew full well she had a lot to do. Whatever it was, it could bloody well wait.

"I'm busy, Sonia. Can this wait?" Arianna kept her back to Sonia as she continued to go through the crates.

"No, Anya, it can't. You've got a visitor. This is Matthew, and he has been asking after you. He wants your advice on something."

Arianna took a deep breath, then released it slowly. She really wasn't in the mood for this. She would rather be left alone. She plastered on a smile and turned to face her pain in the arse best friend and whatever surprise she had this time.

Matthew was a gorgeous, six-foot, brown-eyed stud, and to top it off, he had dimples. But that was it. She noticed these things as any living, breathing female would, but they did absolutely nothing for her. His eyes, though—they held something Arianna refused to delve into.

Sonia had been doing this for months now; trying to set

her up with hotties in the hope Arianna would truly forgive her for the balls up of a date in Greece.

But in all honesty, Arianna couldn't muster up the energy to be interested. She had given her whole heart to Arcaeus, so there just wasn't anything left to give.

Arianna held out her hand. "Hi, Matthew, I'm Arianna. Nice to meet you. I'm afraid Sonia has brought you here under false pretences." She fixed a scathing look at her best friend. Sonia's pout showed how put out she was.

"I'm not the type of girl you want, but I'm sure Sonia has a few more ladies she could introduce you to. Good luck." With that said, Arianna turned, clipboard still in hand, and headed toward her office. She'd had enough for the day. All she wanted was to put her comfy clothes on, as well as her huge slippers, and get a hot chocolate so big she could drown in it.

Arianna was almost to her office door when Sonia caught up with her. "Anya, stop! Seriously, what is wrong with you? That is the tenth guy you have turned down since we returned from Greece. I know what happened upset you, but damn it, girl, come on."

If only Sonia knew just how broken she was, and what truly haunted and upset her every moment she spent alone.

Arianna grabbed her handbag and coat and took her time as she thought of a response.

"Sonia, I'm just not interested. What happened in Greece has nothing to do with this. In fact, it made me realise I'm worth more. I want a man to love me for me, muffin top included."

Arianna kissed Sonia on the cheek before walking out of the office and through the museum.

*S*onia watched her best friend head to the exit. She hated that Arianna was in pain. It was obvious whenever she thought no one was watching. She would hold on to the pendants around her neck, clutch at them as if her life depended on it.

Sonia had no intention of giving up though, especially when Mr Handsome had asked for Arianna personally. So, she was going to be sneaky.

"Matthew, I'm so sorry about that. Arianna has been under a lot of stress lately with the exhibit. I hope you won't hold that against her?"

His offered smile had Sonia stunned. "Of course not. I'm sure she has a lot on her mind, but can I be cheeky and ask for her number?"

Sonia smiled back, turned over her clipboard, and grabbed a scrap piece of paper. "I can do better than that." She grinned and started to write, determination leading her actions.

"Here's her address. She doesn't live that far away from the museum." She trusted Matthew with not only her best friend's address, but with her heart too. They had known each other since they were kids, but it was only recently that she had realised he was perfect for Arianna. Yes, she was meddling again, but she wanted her friend to be happy. If only she could get in on that action too.

After she handed over the paper, she watched as Matthew bowed, his hand over his heart.

"I thank you for this. Be happy in knowing I would do anything for Arianna." With that, he turned and walked toward the exit, his footsteps eating up the route Arianna had taken. Sonia smiled, chivalry wasn't dead after all.

Sonia released a sigh and turned to look up at a fresco of a handsome warrior, sword in hand, in the heat of battle.

"If only. Every girl wants to be rescued." She grinned and patted the fresco. "If Aphrodite did exist, I would definitely ask her for one of you, handsome." She chuckled to herself as she made her way back to her office, oblivious to the fact a certain goddess had indeed been listening.

36

Arianna slammed the door closed and leaned against it, her eyes squeezing shut. Damn, she hated it, really hated it, when Sonia tried to match her up with someone. She didn't need or want the help. She was happy as she was. Happy being miserable. She grumbled about meddling best friends, dumped her bag in the lounge, and headed to the bedroom.

She tied her hair up in a ponytail, donned her favourite pyjamas, and grabbed her Kindle on her way to the lounge. She wanted a cup of tea, and then she was going to lose herself in the world of the Lore. Her favourite books by Kresley Cole always helped her relax.

Arianna opened her Kindle, ready to be engrossed, when her doorbell rang. The chime echoed throughout her apartment.

"Dammit! Sonia, this had better not be you. I'm in no mood to deal with you right now." Arianna's tirade continued as she wrenched the door open, only to stop mid-sentence as she faced her visitor. The stud from the museum was at her door. He looked at her with those gorgeous brown eyes that seemed so familiar.

"Hi, I'm so sorry to bother you at home," he said, his words rushed out, voice deep, "but I really need to speak with you regarding something."

Matthew's eyes were warm and kind as he smiled down at her, his hand held out in greeting. "I was hoping we could start fresh? Hi, I'm Matthew."

Arianna couldn't help herself; she smiled back and took his hand. "Certainly. Hi, Matthew. I'm Dr Arianna Preston."

His hand engulfed hers for just a little longer than necessary before he reluctantly released it.

"A pleasure to meet you, Doctor. I'm after some help with this." He took out a small bag from his pocket and pulled out a small pendant. Arianna's hand shot to her throat as she felt for her own pendants.

"Where did you get that?" Arianna asked, her voice almost a whisper. His smile as she looked up at him for an answer made her heart flutter.

"Can't you read it, Arianna?" His use of her first name made Arianna jerk. The way he said it and how he looked at her was just so familiar. Arianna nodded and bent her head over his hand to read the inscription. She read the words out loud.

"Aphrodite, Goddess of Love, blesses the union between her priest and priestess. With your hearts and souls, love always. Soul mates parted always find each other through time. So I have said, so be it. Blessed Be."

Arianna's eyes shot to Matthew's as she finished reading the inscription. The crinkles in the corner of his eyes made her gasp as recognition finally caught up with her.

His smile almost knocked her off her feet, but his next words cracked and demolished the ice that surrounded her heart. Tears started to trickle, then cascaded down her cheeks.

"Arianna, my *Theia*, didn't I say I would find you? I will always find you."

Arianna's hand covered her mouth, her voice on the verge of becoming a sob. "Arcaeus?"

His smile was all the confirmation Arianna needed before she launched herself into his arms. Their mouths met in a flurry of kisses, showing, without words, the love they felt for one another.

Soul mates would always find each other, whether through time or distance. Or even death.

It was a concept many would never know, but the goddess would agree that love really does conquer all.

⚛

*A*phrodite smiled wide as she watched her priestess and the warrior embrace. All had turned out as she had wanted and expected. Now all that was left was to see to Mr Bachelor himself. She grinned as her faithful friend landed next to her.

"Is Cosmos settled?"

With a small nod, Meton answered, "Yes, my lady. Settled and in the exact place you wanted him."

Aphrodite beamed in response and turned away from the happy couple.

"Good, Meton, and thank you again, old friend. Let us be off and leave the mortals for now. I have a feeling Cosmos may indeed need our help before his trials and tribulations are through."

"Very well, my lady. As you wish."

Aphrodite and her faithful companion, unseen by any and

all mortals, disappeared in a flash of light, a sweet smell of narcissus the only remnant of her visit.

SOULFATE BOOK 2 SOULMATE SERIES
NOW AVAILABLE

She never saw him coming

Sonia's life had become a series of bad dates and lonesome nights. Not one could compare to the warriors of old depicted in the relics she restored.

But when the stone comes to life and her dream guy is here in the flesh, can she handle everything that comes with a forever kind of love?

He should kill her, not protect her

Punished for an act of kindness and locked away for centuries, Cosmos returns to a world he doesn't recognize, and a woman who takes his breath away.

When a prophecy unfolds he will have to make an impossible choice. Protect the woman his soul aches for, or save the world. He can't have both.

SOULDEATH BOOK 3 SOULMATE SERIES
NOW AVAILABLE

He won't watch her die again. Even if it costs his own life.

Hades, lord of the dead, has been forced to watch the world from below for eons. He craves the one thing he doesn't have, can never have… love. Even worse, he is forced to watch his soulmate reincarnated only to die alone without him, over and over.

Not this time. Enough is enough. This time he'll stop her dying even if it defies the fates. Even if it means his own death, he will risk anything for his love.

She's not who she thinks she is. She never has been.

Andromeda has always been in the outside looking in. The odd loner who didn't fit in anywhere. Dreams of the past haunt her and a chance encounter with a dark stranger set her on a different path. She knows him, but she's never met him before. How can she believe his wild claims when she can't even trust her own dreams.

One thing she knows for certain… her life is about to change. Only the fates will decide if its for the better.

ALSO BY J THOMPSON

Soulmate Series
SoulKiss #1
SoulFate #2
SoulDeath #3

Trinity Series
Ebony #1

Dark Desire Series
Dark Confusion #1
Dark Need #2

Paranormal Security Service
Guarding Katelyn #1

Tears of Havoc Series
Cupid's Essence #1

Co-Authored
Dragon fire & Phoenix Ash with Mina Carter
Raanar with Mina Carter

Magic and Mayhem universe
Kracken's Hole Book #1 -Witch out of Water
Kracken's Hole Book #2- Tail of a Witch
Kracken's Hole Book #3- Witch Out of Luck

Elemental Dragon Series
Earth Dragon's Claim #1

Science Fiction Romance
Betraying Ko'ran #1

Stand Alone's
Exercise in Love

ABOUT THE AUTHOR

J. Thompson is a USA Today Bestselling Author of Paranormal and Sci-Fi romance and a major fan of procrastination. Jenn has always loved history, so using her wild imagination and tying in her love of history and fantasy, she began a new adventure into the world of words. Weaving romance into old worlds and giving life to her mythical inspired novels is what Jenn does best, and she has a lot more planned in the future, including some hard assed demons. When she isn't bent over her laptop with the crazy writer eyes, you will find Jenn making jewellery, cross stitching and it doing paper crafts. Jenn is also an avid lover old skool skills like archery and sword fighting.

Maybe a touch nuts Jenn is an author who believes wholeheartedly that people are good and that everyone deserves romance - even Hades.

Connect with Jean online at www.soulmatenovels.com

For regular updates sign up to Jenns Newsletter HERE

Printed in Great Britain
by Amazon